From the genesis of pristine greatness, from the bosom of certainty of role and place and function, the stories of **BROTHERHOOD OF THE SPURS** move with Dutch slaver to St. Martin, Caribbean island, but, in microcosm, macrocosm, murmuring the history, toward the future, from degradation to hope of reparation.

You will find the Black woman, African Diaspora woman. See her on center stage, draped in shadow yet baseline, background but ever present. You will find the evocation of primal pain in the interspersed primal passions, simple joys.

Always there is the ever-present thinking, unifying thread; always there is the presence of a quality of spirituality; and for the future, a search for humanness, transcending difference, and the poignancy of a monument to ancestral memory.

In the microcosmic macrocosm of St. Martin, in the unending cycle of souls and generations, here Sekou attempts a meeting point.

> – Pearl Eintou Springer
>   *Director*
>   National Heritage Library
>   Republic of Trinidad & Tobago

BOOKS BY HOUSE OF NEHESI PUBLISHERS

Skin
Drisana Deborah Jack

Cul-de-Sac People
A St. Martin Family Series
Mathias S. Voges

The Salt Reaper
Poems from the flats
Lasana M. Sekou

Friendly Anger
The Rise of the Labor Movement in St. Martin
Joseph H. Lake, Jr.

Salted Tongues
Modern Literature in St.Martin
Fabian Adekunle Badejo

The Essence of Reparations
Amiri Baraka

The House That Jack Built and Other Plays
Louie Laveist

Same Sea ... Another Wave
Cynthia Wilson

Words Need Love Too
Kamau Brathwaite

Regreso, regreso al hogar - Conversaciones II
La educación occidental y el intelectual Caribeño
George Lamming

Pass It On! A Treasury of Virgin Islands Tales
Jennie N. Wheatley

Illegal Truth
Ras Changa

Masquerade
Ian Valz

Brotherhood
OF THE
SPURS

Lasana M. Sekou

House of Nehesi Publishers
P.O. Box 460
Philipsburg, St. Martin
Caribbean

www.houseofnehesipublish.com

© 2007, 1997 by Lasana M. Sekou.
All rights reserved.
ISBN: 9780913441862
LC Control Number: 2006937555

Cover graphics design by Suzette Moses-Burton
Cover painting by Virgilio Mendez, 1996, private collection
Photography: Island Photo Studio/P. Gunn, Saltwater
Collection/M. Illidge. Promo graphics by S.L DesignMedia.

For Jacqui & Judy

Contents

	page
Introduction	ix
A Salting	1
The Wake	39
Brotherhood of The Spurs	93
Firespill	130
Glossary	165

INTRODUCTION

Brotherhood of The Spurs is the second collection of short stories by the brilliant Caribbean poet and storyteller, Lasana M. Sekou. *Love Songs Make You Cry* (1989) was the first compilation of short stories to have been written by Sekou as well as the first such publication ever by a writer from his Caribbean homeland of St. Martin.

In this second volume, Sekou has carefully honed his writer's skills as he moves from a short story format firmly rooted in the oral tradition to one which draws more heavily upon the conventions of a mini-novella. In this expansion of technique, this gifted writer has taken on even greater literary challenges, perhaps most evident in his experimentation with rather complex temporal transitions. The stories are fashioned more of dialogue and less of description and explanation, which brings their characters more vividly to life by allowing them to do the actual storytelling. Moreover, whereas the first volume of short stories focused most heavily on character development *per se*, this collection explores more closely some of the situational and relational contexts in which individuals may find themselves. In so doing, Sekou faithfully exposes both the hypnotic rhythms and richly-hued tapestry of Caribbean life.

The first story, "A Salting," is an historically informed piece, a literary monument to the nobility and dignity of the author's African ancestors. It is a masterful relating of two very different journeys in the life of an Ashanti womanchild of noble parentage who comes of age during her passage to a new world.

The story is thoroughly permeated with powerful imagery and profound symbolism, most notably surrounding the "stolen" fertility of the young African woman. Its brute focus on the violation of the essential humanity of an innocent child so bursting with promise indelibly impresses upon the reader the sheer horror of slavery. A subtle linking of past with present also courses throughout, evident in the description of simple hand greetings, in the verbal communication among strangers, as much as in the clandestine lagoon delivery of new "slaves." The young woman's christening by salt water during her sea journey to the Americas will have particularly poignant resonance with St. Martiners, whose parents, grandparents, and great-grandparents worked the salt pans of Great Bay and Grand Case. In all, "A Salting" is a deeply moving testament to the talents and contributions, suffering and sacrifice, tremendous courage and resilience of the Afro-Caribbean peoples.

The second story, "The Wake," is a psychological study which explores male-female relations and examines in particular the corroding effects of violence upon innocent and culpable alike. In it we see the re-emergence and maturation of Sekou's favorite love theme as he extols the redeeming power of love of and commitment to family and country, and celebrates the healing power of patience and forgiveness, which together guide one of the story's main characters to ultimate redemption.

Structurally speaking, the most complex of

the four stories, "The Wake" mimics the revelationary nature of self-discovery through a series of carefully crafted flashbacks. As a literary technique, these flashbacks further serve to grip the reader tightly in anticipatory suspense . . . until the final release. In the process, the story provides a representative life history typical of many St. Martin men and their families during the early part of the twentieth century. The tale is also liberally sprinkled with astute socio-political insights into contemporary St. Martin, evidence that the political scientist and journalist side of Sekou is never far beneath the surface.

The third story, "Brotherhood of The Spurs," is very much a cultural piece in its examination of cockfighting as a popular Caribbean pastime. Cockfighting is itself thoroughly infused with rich symbolism. An illegal activity throughout many parts of the Caribbean, cockfighting represents a flaunting at official "colonial" and "neo-colonial" authority. As such, it is an expression of resistance, of might, of "manhood" even, in a society wherein the most modest of ambitions are readily frustrated.

As is the case with many other sports, cockfighting is also often a symbolic enactment of an existing rivalry and safety-valve venting of tension, and—somewhat ironically—a concomitant uniting of individuals and peoples across other, sometimes externally imposed, lines of division. In the story this is manifest in the friendly "French" St. Martin/Guadeloupe rivalry between two island peoples territorially, linguistically and culturally unique, historically thrust together by colonial politics and now intricately linked by family ties. As Sekou notes:

> Around this triad *(of seated cockfight officials)*, sealed in place and time by a rite of the medicine woman's eyes, were circles deep of families forged by centuries, and friendships forged through life-long days, and blood, and political alliances. And those circles spread out to encircle more families and acquaintances and villages and visitors and made space across from the brotherhood nucleus to the challengers, kindred in the game and in the region of engagement.

This story thus represents a culmination of Sekou's love theme, an appeal to the notion of brotherhood which, one might argue, constitutes the highest and truest form of love. As such, it is a call to those ties which unite, truly befitting the signature piece of the collection.

"Firespill," the final story of the volume,

takes the form of a futuristic political commentary. In it, the author imagines the fulfillment of the St. Martin dream of unification of the currently bi-national, half-"Dutch" half-"French" 37-square-mile island of St. Martin. The resulting attempt to envision the attendant processes of decolonization in a time of increasing globalization renders a Caribbean scenario vaguely Orwellian but one much less sinister . . . or is it so? What would the true cost of economic, and thereby political, independence be? Who will pay the price and at what cost? Will the necessary sacrifice ultimately be worth it? The tale is clearly more than mere whimsical speculation.

In playfully extending the inherent logic of current globalizing trends and independence drive, Sekou addresses issues of substantial topical concern; the resulting juxtaposition of fancifulness and seriousness mixed with vague allusion to various shadowy evils keeps the reader ever off-balance, intrigued and very much in suspense. In subtly teasing the St. Martin readers about their attitudes toward the diverse "others" within their midst, he quietly reminds his fellow compatriots that theirs is a proud legacy of cooperation and mutual respect forged out of painful adversity. And finally, in proudly depicting a sun-kissed memorial of atonement dedicated to the region's African (and East Indian) ancestral peoples, he effectively reconciles present, future, and past, until suddenly, with a raising of eyebrow, greeting of stiffened fingers, and twinkle in his eye, Sekou gently pulls the reader full circle.

Sekou's poetic narratives are spellbinding. His stories are compelling, beautifully and powerfully written, rich in fertile imagery and symbolic allusions, well-fortified by "national" reference and socio-political commentary. Phrases such as "The air polished the lighted tip *(of his cigar)* with embers of silence" and "He clamped his body around Pearl like a soldier's helmet covered with a dreaded net of locks" aptly illustrate the degree to which his poetry underscores his prose and serves to fully engage the reader as active participant in his story-telling. Other original locutions, such as "he rolled and holstered the paper under his left arm" or "*(with)* rheumatism sneering in his joints as he spoke," once expressed, could not conceivably have been formulated otherwise and become forever etched in the reader's memory.

An accomplished poet and dedicated cultural worker from the northeastern Caribbean, Sekou is best known for his numerous volumes of poetry and dramatic performances. With this latest, masterful foray into a new form of artistic expression, however, this talented author has irrefutably proven himself a rapidly rising star in the bright firmament of Caribbean writers.

– Dr. Joanna W. A. Rummens
Centre for Research on Latin America and the Caribbean (CERLAC)
Toronto, Canada

A SALTING

Nana Mandisa told her that she would be made ready before the winds of reddish dust rushed out to cover the Great Sea and paint the far horizon with the fertile rouge soot cleansed from God's Land.

Nana Mandisa told her she was nearing her time; that she was lucky to be cleansed for the first time with the great land; and that wherever in this world the first harvesting of a girl's ripen blood mixed with water and washed over land, there would her eternal home be.

"Child of mine," teased the girl's mother that night, "if you keep listening to Nana Mandisa, you will go crazy just like her. She has no children. That is probably why she left her country and kinfolk so long ago.

"I see you visit her daily these days. Do you forget you are my only child? Soon you will want to go off with her and see this world she has you raving about. She will petition on your behalf and persuade us that it is your destiny to see this world in her company."

The city's people, who gave the old woman the title Nana, said the elder was touched not by madness but by God, so that the ancestors of many folk could guide her in weaning special children from the immaculate birth of virgin mothers. No citizen wanted to say that she was a seer, though she was always right in foretelling the time a selected girl's first bleeding would ready her for the seed of man and woman's most ancient labor.

"Sure, my wide-eyed-tickle-of-a-daughter," said the girl's father the other morning, "Nana Mandisa is inspired to select a girl to foretell of her time. She puts this time in you. You believe. It is close to the rites of your age group. So it happens. Anyway, that is the secret business of women, and you have Queen Mother, mother, aunts, and sisters to prepare you."

After a pause and puzzled creasing around his mouth, he continued. "And that story of blood and water, where did she unearth such a tale? Maybe it comes from the people of Yemoja. At her age, she goes and comes as she pleases, and brings what stories suit her madness.

"Her features tell the world that she is of the People of Heaven who tenant the south, but I have been told of no such story among them. As for you, Nana Mandisa will surely see your blood when you bring more sons to water the fold of this family. I tell you, she will live that long. Longer than all of us."

The father leaned forward. The daughter, sitting on her hips with legs slung closed and away from her upper body, straightened almost to a kneel on the orange-over-black-dyed straw mat. He softly touched the back of his right hand fingers to the young forehead, as if timing her blood flow. He uttered in the voice with which he pronounced judgment at court that he was off to the council, that today he would vote to advance the apprenticeship of the senior member's eldest son. The son would now be able to go and study at the king's court.

With a sweep of authority, the judge gathered about his body the clothing of cotton and sacred animal skin, the vestment of his office.

"That young man will make a just law-giver in his time," he reflected.

The girl rose before her father, waited until he passed, and followed imitatively—hands clasped behind her back, head down as if in thought.

"A just law-giver," repeated the father. This time his voice raised to the pitch with which he called one of his four wives.

Once her mother, the youngest wife, asked the daughter in earshot of the patriarch if she did not find the apprentice handsome. Her mother was well-known for her expressive manners in speech and gestures and for her eyes that sparkled with the likeness of a thousand fiery crushed stars.

"Is he not handsome," she inquired casually, "with skin so manly sable, it is the night, and teeth so unblemished that they reflect the pure smiles of his ancestors?"

Her father presented a conspiratorial smile, leaned over then too and felt the child's forehead with the back of his right hand fingers.

"The boy's father has fine sons. It is a good family," he said matter-of-factly to his fourth wife—the one who yet dazzled him to youthful indulgence with her bright charm of eyes.

The girl had glanced at the young man once or twice as he genuflected before her father while visiting her family's compound. She did not know when or where she had overheard that before the season of rains was over, he would be going to the royal compound of learning in Kumasi. There he would study further the laws of the kingdom as well as the languages of the peoples from across the Sahara who traded dates, cloth, utensils, and salt in her city for kola nuts, gold, and sometimes slaves. When humans—in debt, for crime, or from war—were sold in the market, her father's sullen and angered face would silence his compound. Sometimes there was a mourning silence for days. Somehow, she felt, he mumbled his disdain for the trade in bondage only in his compound, and strangely, only when she sat before him as she so loved to do.

She did hear, too, that in the course of his new studies, the apprentice would be inducted into mysteries—manners of the soul, communion with ancestors, division of the seasons, hidden ways and spirits of the elements that constitute the world and the heavens, systems of building, cures for ailments, the paths of reasoning, and other secrets, some not to be thought of by children or spoken by women. He would learn the language of gold weights and trade duties, official manners of addressing, and customs of peoples from the Great Sea's coast and of the principal forest states ruled by her Asanthane, Osei Tutu.

She knew, and was somehow excited, about the apprenticeship being fulfilled, to use her father's pronouncement, "in this tenth year of the blessed reign."

At the slightest prompting, when surrounded by his four wives, thirty-seven children, extended relations, and ever-blooming garden of grand and great-grandchildren over which he doted, the patriarch would surely follow the "blessed reign" pronouncement with: "When a king has good counselors, his reign is peaceful."

In the silence that followed whenever the sire spoke of the blessed and peaceful reign, the daughter always felt that the whole family felt as she—breathlessly happy and proud of her father, prominent in the Mmerante, a counselor of laws to the Asanthane.

Her father loved traveling as much as he took pride in being a just and worldly law-giver. He lamented, however, that his travels—always with one of his wives and three of his sons—were mostly on summons to the Great House of the Asanthane to give the monarch account of laws and judgments passed among the people and merchants of the city.

The girl's father loved travelers too, and it was the tales from distances that endeared Nana Mandisa to him. Despite the talk about her madness, it was he who sought her out most, to be blessed with stories of the peoples of God's Land. The stories he eked out of traders who reached the city by foot, beasts of burden, and river craft were meager compared to the trove of tall tales, news and views Nana Mandisa brought from the nations that summoned her for special healing and mostly to bring forth the children foretold by priests, prophets, and omens, by a cast of cowry shells and divining bones on hollowed earth, or by the appearance of falling stars and other heavenly signs.

"But this blood and water story, why has she not told me of this one before she told you, my precious last-born?" The daughter giggled at the exaggerated tone of childish curiosity woven into her father's otherwise stately voice.

Yet when it came to pass shortly thereafter that Nana Mandisa visited the judge's compound and asked permission for the girl to be her companion down the river—to bring forth a promised and immaculate birth for a coastal people who were legendary in their defiance of inland kings and armies—the final episode of the three-day negotiation was the telling of the origin of the blood and water story.

Her father emerged in the center of the compound's foreyard. He was holding and patting both hands of the old traveler in his. His face was somewhat saddened. At the entrance of his family's compound, the patriarch called for his last-born with a gesture of the hand. Her mother, who had been looking from her doorway, sent the child with an approving tap on the shoulder. The child skipped to the father and was drawn into the elders' *grande tenue*.

The judge bowed before Nana Mandisa.

"Mother of Journeys, we are of one generation. Yet, before your tales I am but a child turning in the womb of my living mother. This story, blood and water, is indeed older than we."

He paused.

"Wisdom be unto you. My daughter is your daughter, for it is you who brought forth many of my children from the wombs of my wives, alive. Who else can come for this young blessing blossoming between us if not you?" He touched the child's forehead with the back of his right hand's fingers.

"If she becomes a woman on this journey, it is you who will see her blood matter washed with water and make the earth where she sees her time a different place. May your ancestors and the forebears of my household and kindred lay the path beneath your feet. May the attendant divinities keep the waters without trouble. The Omnipotent One alone will cast light upon destiny. Guidance."

The girl, excited about going on her first far journey, could hear no more words as the two elders wrapped her in the cosmos of ancient sayings and customs of speech. When her father raised his hand to the old woman in the salute of agreement and peace, her mother's voice, pitched to a song, rang out.

"Come, child of mine! Prepare yourself to follow Nana Mandisa to her home. Tomorrow you will leave before the first light of dawn to a new place. Come, here are your finely-woven clothes. Come, the currency for your expenses is gathered.

"Come, you will take yam for God and deities. There is food to share with Nana Mandisa, your companions and servants, and the kin and good people you will surely meet. Here are clothes for wrapping and sleeping, and to tell the world of your family and land. You will take water to quench your thirst. Take this sweet bush and these fragrant oils for your bath and the smoothing of your oh-so-pure skin.

"Were you a woman, you would have your hair dressed appropriate to your age. Were you a wife, you would be adorned with jewels of gold and so on for this journey. It is as well, let the world know you are a child. Our children can go far into any country with means of their own and without trouble.

"Oh look," swooned the mother, "your sisters are coming to greet you and help you carry your packing to the home of Nana Mandisa. Well, well, well, they are bringing gifts from their mothers."

The girl rushed to meet her sisters. Her mother was begrudged somewhat for showing off whenever good fortune came her way, but the child was favored in her father's compound. Her sisters surrounded her with laughter and giggles and pushing and pulling and all of that which sisters do at such a time when happiness for one overcomes any wish that it she who had been bestowed the gift.

"Well, look at that if you please! Tsk, tsk, tsk. You did not fall from the sky at all. You are well-loved. And oh-so-pretty-pretty! Just as my mother was. My hand is clean, and I am sending kisses for you: smack, smack, smack!

"Come, come, come child of mine. Have you forgotten your name already? Are you deaf to your own mother's voice? Nana Mandisa will not wait on you forever, you know. Please, precious child of mine, make haste for goodness sake.

"Come and prepare yourself for a washing and a long journey."

The child rose at earliest dawn and roused all in Nana Mandisa's household with news of a dream she had had that restless night. Between the washing, prayers, morning meal, dressing, and final packing, none but Nana Mandisa truly listened to the girl's dream about feasting travelers on an angry river.

"Well, it is a dream that can be for good or bad," said the old woman as she parceled and bundled her herbs and scripture of talismans. That said, the child raised her right eyebrow in that manner when she agreed with parents, family, and friends to cautiously put an issue to end. She dashed off and threw herself into the packing excitement.

Three sentinels sent by her father were waiting: two at a stone hearth, one at the door of Nana Mandisa's dwelling. Five women servants sent by her mother arranged the clothing, food, and gifts for kin, good people, and bartering strangers surely to be met on the way.

Nana Mandisa's nephew overlooked the packing with much laughter and such a fanfare of his hands. He was brought to the city many rainy seasons ago by the old one. She told those who were bound to ask that he was one of her dead sisters' sons. The nephew and the old woman had no looks or ascent of language in common. His skin was nearer to the inflamed afternoon sky that promised a hot tomorrow. Nana Mandisa's hue was of the velvet night. He served his aunt with adoration, as if she had saved him from certain damnation.

The three guardians ate last. Thereafter, the clay bowls were washed. One who identified himself as the head sentinel asked Nana Mandisa's permission to be placed before the travelers, with one of his fellows at the child's side, and one—who stammered without shame—at the back of the group.

Permission granted, the nephew whistled a song which tells of travelers preparing to leave for the unknown. The servants plucked the baskets and bundles from about the abode. With youthful swiftness, each alighted a weight atop the waiting cushion of cloth on her own head. Together they became a grace of leaves, a song of balance, weaved in a seductive breeze that danced them to the foreyard's center. The nephew blew out the lamps and sprayed water from his mouth to out the cooking fire.

All stood ready, chatting, waiting for Nana Mandisa. Mother of Journeys appeared, paused at the entrance of her dwelling, the child's head fretting through the cloth falling over the elder's akimbo right hand. What kept the old woman for what seemed to a child so long at the door? The anxious, wide-eyed youth saw nothing that could prevent the journey.

The old doctor walked assuredly, and still with a touch of hesitancy, to the waiting party. She placed herself amidst the vibrant brace of young people. The child was practically busheled under her arm in the wraps of cloth that warded off the cool, freshly crisp forest breeze of morning's first yawn.

When the group reached the river, greetings passed between them and other travelers. Soon all assembled on the vessel. It pressed hungrily through the water, reigned by its captain and crew.

First it was the fragrance of crisp early morning, then the sting of salt while passing the marketplace, which was now coming alive, too. Now the senses of the child were being rushed through with the dew of dawn's last breath and the potpourri of fresh and earthy and green and wooded smells carried along with the river, and of the river itself.

The river's movement, as a slowly stirring body of magical fullness, trembled her belly and lower back. Nana Mandisa looked upon her, and she was comforted. Down the mighty road of river, the water craft coursed. There were laughter and melee and songs of praise to the Creator, divinities, and ancestors, and for the fineness of the morning.

As the sun climbed over the headdress of trees, drummers pounded, while flutists and other players of instruments joined in the artful orchestration for life's sake. The symphony, now attended by a groom of singers, pealed birds from their nesting, danced them in a circle above the craft and scattered them in frightful delight. Calls of the forest confirmed the awakening of day. Some travelers peeled layers of clothing off to reveal the wet shining of skin. The sentinels went off to pass time with other warriors of their age who were accompanying travelers of means.

The first town took an eternal morning to appear, to answer the anticipation of the child. The people who lighted the shore wore clothing with new markings. Scripts on their faces told of their clan, status, tribe, state, and region. "As those of my father tell of my people and customs," answered Nana Mandisa to the child's whispered inquiries.

While stuffing the child's finger in rolls of cloth to subdue her pointing, the older head made way for a long-necked young woman with a princess's pouting of bare breasts. The child pulled her finely-flowered wrap tighter around her two barely visible blossoms. Princess neck sat next to the old lady. Silence followed the formal greeting among the passengers. Silence followed the seating and standing of the people from the new port. Silence lasted until the craft was well-centered between the thighs of land. Above, the headdress of trees reached with glad tidings for the heavens.

The travelers from both ports spoke only to their own companions, in lowered voices, eyeing others from calm distances.

The drummers began to tap the sound of their own style and school and nation with fetal heart tenderness.

Nana Mandisa smiled a "wait-and-see-something" at the child, then at the elegant young woman. Neither offered back a smile.

As drummers drew themselves into a heated beating, talking-sounds molested the borders of silence and overcame the hushed voices.

One trader from the first port opened her basket of spices, picked out a sample, rose noisily, and bumped her bubbly self past the child with a swish and said, "Forgive me." She headed for a fancy bundle of coiffured women from the second port.

Soon all of the trading women were pitching at each other with salutation and goods; selling and debating; frowning and sucking their teeth; jutting their hands akimbo and laughing like sisters. A well-spring of fraternity engulfed the passengers and they exchanged news and made inquiries about each other's states and clans and the known world. The child felt like she was with her sisters at the city's marketplace.

The sentinels, who had returned to their posts upon arrival at the second port, ventured off again to join members of their own age, and then to fellow warriors from the second port. These they greeted stiffly with hands and fingers, showed body markings—some of which marked manhood, others of which were glyphs of lineage, yet others of which chronicled war—and displayed their weapons of wood and iron and bronze and handles of ivory and gold mixtures that carried with them the scent of value and color. No one touched the other's weapons, for there could be strong magic about. But for sure, some coveted them with eyes of wonder and other such feelings that are known to fester causes for war among men.

The elderly men exchanged kola nuts, dates, and palm wine. Then they invited each other to play the board games that welded their nations into one region. They debated, first strongly, then with the scratchy teasing laughter of old men who had had enough of war. Their debate was about the rules of the game that each nation carved to its liking and benefit. Soon the peace-gifting of kola nuts and dates, the laughing spirit of the palm, and the sweetness of the game overcame the limits of rules. They played as one country.

The child curiously eyed the few other children. Some, like she, were tucked to the side of an adult. Others were asleep or babbling while strapped to the back or front of their mothers' bodies. She leaned on the closest breast of old Nana, who was listening attentively to The Stately One beside her. Some of the young woman's words were new, some were like the child's language.

When the relate was done, Nana Mandisa told the child that The Stately One was soon to be wedded and was her people's pride dancer. She was accompanying other dancers, musicians, singers, sportsmen, and ambassadors to a sister nation. There the royal heir would be called forth to speak his right to serve as chief. If accepted, according to the tradition of his people, there would be an inaugural feast from one moon to the next.

The girl peeked across at the dancer. The Stately One looked aside at the glow of cuteness and playfully danced her right eyebrow up and down. The child flicked her eyebrow in instant response, astonished that a stranger could do as she thought only she and her mother could. The dancer opened her eyes and mouth in equal astonishment. Her smile blossomed like morning's glory, inviting the child to admire her front-center parting of upper polished row of ivory teeth, set in black gums behind a feminine full of equally black lips.

The stately dancer spoke to Nana Mandisa in an inquiring and more humbled tone. The girl knew this tone. She, too, was taught how to speak before elders without appearing too fast and without manners.

Nana Mandisa answered that they were off to one end of God's Land from where they would see an endless water, the Great Sea over which the sun passes to sleep. Yes, this was the child's first travel from mother's dwelling and compound of her father. Yes, it was a destined journey to see the world.

The Stately One frowned. The skin between her eyebrows crushed into folds like the red funeral cloth draped on bodies of grief. The child sifted through the words spoken haltingly to Nana Mandisa: of strange people who traveled in large dwellings upon the water without their women, smelled of rotten flesh, grew boils and extra hair on their faces, had fiery eyes, and the skin of those who cannot walk long in sunlight, sported hair of the monkey and mouths without lips, wore clothes that hid most of their bodies and knee-high shoes of animal skin, and carried weapons that spit fire like those paraded by Asanthane's select guardians.

Nana Mandisa answered that she knew of this trouble moving over God's Land; and that in her travels northward from her father's abode, she had heard how a great Matamba queen had battled these strangers, was probably still fighting them; and that as for those strangers, they need not be feared as they are only another kind of human.

The dancer made a startled inquiry and spoke so rapidly that the child did not understand a word.

"Yes, I came from deep down in God's Land, while I was of marriageable age. And, anyway," continued Mother of Journeys, "we are all still within the kingdom of Asanthane. He is making peace and riches for so many. He defeated the Denkyira in The Battle of Feyiase.

"Your chief is one of the six or so, once suspicious of each other, who pledged his state to the Asanthane, that the Great He may rule rightly from the Golden Stool. Now victory belongs to those who belong. We are in a good country. It is still true, I tell you, a Brong man can visit the Fante so many miles away. There he will receive food and hospitality from a perfect stranger who is of his clan.

"Anyway, we shall not be at that western end of the world long enough to meet with troublesome strangers, nor with those who help them steal humans from God's Land."

"Then be blessed, Nana, with a good journey," smiled the dancer, trying to speak fully in the child's language.

The child was gently rocked to sleep by the great river's washing palms of water at craft-side. Fading were the word-sounds of drums joined by singers, dancers, flute players, the servants, the nephew . . . all the peoples encircled by the rhythm of life upon the craft.

"Curses upon you, devil's spawn!

"Be damned!" The shrill, choking cry of an old familiar voice cracked into the child's sleep.

Her eyes were molested open. The rhythm upon the water had stopped. Nana Mandisa was wrapping her tightly in her doctor's clothing. Her hands shoved and tucked and sought to bound the child away with fevered madness. Her breasts were bare and boiling and buttery, hanging heavily around the back of the child's neck like blazing logs.

Wails and curses and languages and blood

and bleeding from holes in bodies and the smell of burning . . . What was that burning? Not like wood or stone or animal skin or meat or fruits or yam or milk or grass, or gold as explained by her father.

The burning scraped tears from her eyes. She felt the left breast skin of old Nana swell. The swelling burst and mixed with aged blood and burnt and salted uncooked flesh, and it all rushed to hide in her ears that could not hear, in pores and eyes and nostrils and mouth and tongue, and lodged between her teeth and gums, and choked down her throat . . . and . . . her eyes could see no more . . . or knew not what she was seeing.

She heard her mother's voice: "Our children can go far . . . without trouble."

The sentinel placed at her side grabbed her shoulders, shook her: "Little sister in my charge, run. I will find you to the end of time . . . protect you . . . my vow to your father."

"Take her! Make haste!" said the rear guard, his stammering overcome.

The girl blinked and bulged her blood-washed eyes looking for Nana Mandisa but saw her not. For sure the motionless weight both sentinels were dragging off her was not Nana

Mandisa. Neither was she that heaviness that tumbled over and gaped a gash of broken flesh, breathless, faceless, breastless. And that part of the dead weight which looked like the private portal of womanhood that the sentinels had tried to hurriedly cover with rags barely the color of Nana Mandisa's clothing could never belong to her Nana anyway.

With one hand, the head sentinel dragged the child to her buckling feet and pushed The Stately One, who had lost all speech, onto, into, over the child as a shield.

"Make haste!" he roared, swung around, found his spear in a warrior's dance, lodged it into the neck of a creature, lipless, hairless. That creature fell but a clouded prism of others charged.

He continued cutting through skins that changed color from slash to slash, raging through garments known and unknown. Then his spear hit upon metal as a rap on an enemy's door found in a thicket. A bursting sound answered from the metal's mouth, or was it its eye? It brought closer the burnt odor and stifling smoke that was grating into the child's eyes. The warrior fell backward. A red fountain punctured him. A foot, wrapped high to the knee in hardened animal skin, rose and crushed down on the pots of flesh where ancestors keep in men all generations gone and those to come.

As suddenly, the crusher's face went from triumphant monkey gnashing teeth to a bloodletting waterfall. The friendly market woman, appearing out of nowhere, had retrieved and lanced the fallen warrior's spear across the middle of the troublesome stranger's face.

The personal guardian pushed the girl and the speechless one, clutching to one another, over the craft's nearest side. The belly of water was gone. They were received by a land's thigh of rocks and sticks and blood and bodies tied and torn, and bodies moaning, still, and bleeding through. The girl's face slapped the rocky earth with a jagged sting that stole the light and sound and smell and taste, and the touching of life. The horror of stillness embalmed her.

*****

Leaving the drowsiness of her fright, the child's consciousness struggled to meet wakefulness with a breathless smile of disbelief. Sleep tossed her from its nightmare-riddled bosom. She would, she thought, be caught safely in

Nana's golden stool of a lap and cushioned in her ample garden of breasts.

She willed her arms to be tossed around the elder. The child wanted the wakefulness that relieved the nightmares of being kidnapped by evil spirits, those secret nightmares that assailed her sleep when mother was the wife to accompany father to audience with the king.

Her arms would not move. Her feet refused her. Her eyes opened but refused light and were being picked into as with the thorns that drew blood from the feet of playing children.

Her ears prickled back at the pain of her eyes. She heard wailing and calling and moans and groans and the choking of tears and phlegm of coughing, and repeating of words and songs so much like names and prayers yet so much like madness and the cursing of evil spirits.

The furrowing of her senses in the darkness scowled at the tightening of tender flesh on the left side of her face. It was there, now an oasis of stitching pain, where her head had arrowed her face to slap the river's edge. The prickling twitch of pain began to offer her a backward trough of memory.

Her heart pumped with a strange tightness, burning her insides as air escaped with scalding speed to be replaced by pockets of nothing or something foul and pasted. The smell was upon her now, was her. It was like the stench of piss and shit. No, no, it was more like the fly-beset carcass encountered as she played with friends near the city's food gardens tended by her mother and the other women.

And now there was blood. Blood, dried and raw and a ghost of fumes of flesh cut open for slaughter. A pus of fear pressed like a dull, sawing pain down, up, aside, around, and into her, boiling inward. Her budding of breasts felt like they were bitten away to bar the flow of milk and blood . . . and then reared the taste of old, uncooked meat, anchored in her mouth, wedged and plaqued between her teeth: "NANAMANDISAAAAAAAAAAAAAAAAAAAAAAAA!"

Her breath railed out heaves of choking and no tears and: "NANAAAMANDISAAAAAA!"

Through the blink of silence, parted by her fear, a tortured voice struggled to raise and rattle and drag a clattering of iron in a tired lift of iron and wood: "Little . . . little sister in my . . . charge . . . I will find . . . you . . . to the end . . ."

The gasping torrent of human torment bellowed in on the sentinel's vow. It was as if she had coughed up this torment and now, for its pus-filled awakening, she would be spat into a damned consumption.

The guardian's promise to find her was the blink of hope. It placed her between an infernal, invisible black swaddling of breathing flesh at her sides, at her head, at her feet, above her, below her. The air became fouler. She felt a piddling upon her belly and knew that she was naked but for a cloth bounding her waist tightly and pushing itself between her thighs, knotting at the bottom of her back, from which a new burning was boiling out of her bones.

A steaming stench and a weak weeping from above followed the dripping. A salting sprinkle settled on the child's parched lips and singed through the cracks that started to bleed when she called out to Nana Mandisa. She tasted tears and blood and the piddling and was iron-held there on a rack that was seeding and kneading her back with maggots of splinters.

She lay there, waiting, still hoping that the dripping and sprinkling might be rain. Soon there would be sky and stars and moon, better than all that . . . for with this boiling of heat cramping through the gentle arch of her lower back, it must be day, and she would wake to a darling of unclouded sun.

The dripping upon her belly turned to a hot pushing, lashing of water, slapping all over her.

"Oh-Nana-Mandisa-where-is-this-place?" trembled her voice in frightened squeaks.

She smelled a memory of a cow gushing the hot earth with a steam of yellowish white water from its hindquarters.

"That is the waste of its body, the same as with humans," came her father's voice with stunning clarity.

A howling of curses barked from below. One in her tongue roared with a gnashing rage: "WHO IS PISSING ON ME AGAIN?!"

"Forgive meeeeee." A cry too feeble to be heard down deep, scurried into the abounding blindness.

The child's ears glimpsed memory of the scurrying voice. It had to be the bubbly trader who had bumped past her earlier. The slayer of the head sentinel-killer. The child's stomach turned to empty itself but only a puke of spittle leaked over the corners of her lips. The foul rest swallowed back into her. Her body threw up gestures of cough. Not a sound crawled forth from her.

"Forgive me," shuddered the voice, now so small, unfinished and finished, as a life's last utterance.

The child felt again the boiling at the small of the back. It speared her and was pulled to her belly and then rushed through her with a fire of wild redness while sweat picked and slashed up through her flesh holes. Suddenly, she felt a movement like that of the craft during her bright morning. Was she still on the craft? Still on the river, she wondered.

The fever was lashing with greater fury at the place of her consumption. Her pain collided with an offense of voices from atop, as if spoken from a throat at laughter.

Laughter? she barely thought before her nostrils were forced through with a gale of salt and bushy greenness. Was she back at the river where the dream would end with the laughter she was hearing? Was that the salt brought by camel riders from up in God's Land? Perhaps salt had been brought aboard the craft by traders from a new port while she had slept.

The pain of her face and body was burying her memory of the last morning she knew. The wailing around her was distancing itself from her as if she was going to a new place, not of this world that was refusing her light. Again came the breezy rush bearing the scent of salt, green plants, blossoming flowers, and fruit-laden trees.

And again entered the rush of wind-born salt, budding green, and ripeness . . . and it pushed out a feeling of wetness from between her bruised thighs. It must have been urine, like the cow's on hot earth, or as from the woman trader above a long moment ago.

From beneath, her own language gargled and spat to a burst of lips out of a man's mouth. "WHAT CLOT OF BLOOD IS THIS NOW?!" She was being cursed in her own tongue for the first time in her life! A raging, and flesh pulling on iron and iron rushing to yield naught and the cursing: "IS MY MOUTH TO BECOME THE SHIT HOLE OF THIS GOD-FORSAKEN WORLD?!"

Stranger words and spitting and struggling and unyielding of iron to the silent stretching shrieks and the gasping, dull tearing of flesh gorged filled the air, and moaning from below rose as a sating of prayers for which no blessing of light and release came down.

Crippled tightly under the iron holdings forbidding her movement, she received a gushing of vomit that lunged from one side of her and splattered the darkness, onto bodies wreathing to escape, greasing the iron of sweat, refuse, and mucous-pasted wood. The eruption raised anew the fouling of fetid air.

The sentinel, defying the stench, searching still, caged as the beasts of sacred courage traded in her city's market, called to her, "Little sister in my charge . . . there are coastal peoples down here . . . listen to them. Some speak our language and that of the cursed captors . . . They call our kidnappers makambas and bakras. Some say they will not eat us as others are saying."

"Who are you who speak?" flung a trembling accent of her language. It might have been the nephew, but her body was fevering the ripeness of memory to delirium.

"Why would they search our teeth and tongue as we do animals for slaughter? Tell me that, chief warrior."

"What manner of man, tell me, would handle the cock and seeds of other men with coveting and leering and laughter?"

"And why, why they bite woman breasts to blood?" came the grated voice of another, stitching words of the child's language, as if just for her to hear.

"Sister, drown them out!" commanded the sentinel. "There is no rope to measure the time of this passage through the middle of an underworld. The captors will smuggle some of us through a lagoon by night to a S'maatin Lan'. They will sell us out of the belly of this evil craft as slaves to their own kind."

He rattled now, fending and spearing the obstacles of voices pitching warnings and curses and complaints onto the path his throat-burnt voice had burrowed to her ear holes.

"This vessel is called a slaveship, and is named Snelheid Willem." He coughed and spat a coil of something. "There must be a way back home."

His burrowed cut in the dark, greasing heat was crowding, full of desperate voices sending a last-lick of words and a pitiful calling of names. She recognized holy names and words in her language that were only to be uttered in family shrines. She, too, wanted to pray in the order that she was taught, but the fever boiling from her lower back was consuming her in chaos.

Where the warrior could not fend off the pitiful bawling, he lanced his voice to louder ground: "This morning... when they pitched us with salt water from the Great Sea and whipped us to dance... we saw hills of this S'maatin Lan'. The blessing of green peaks were sweet unto our eyes.

"Some were beaten to the board for calling

out their country's name. Two flung their bodies to embrace the new land and dropped into the sea.

"One was dragged from the water with an iron hook. The other tore his throat from the hook. His body sank. His blood boiled up. The waves were the blood's caisson to the white bottom rim of hills.

"When you know this land, run far into it. No land or time is without hiding places. I will find you . . ."

The sentinel's voice clapped and burst into the voice of many voices shouting and more crying than the child had ever heard. It all sounded like warnings, pleas, and telling one to another what to do, what to do, what to do . . . languages broken and borrowed. It was as if all were building a compound of tongues in that night of the lost tribe of nations upon barracoon waters.

From next to her came a voice, sound-defiant and dim. It pried through the panic din that swayed woefully like a funeral's farewell to a great one.

"Child-of-Nana'andisa."

The voice dragged itself to a corrosive echo, subdued only by jagging, stretching, nail-toothed finger-pointing, reaching, scratching, clawing, gouging for her hand—which hand she knew not in this void of direction. Even when the clawing, as if sensing her recoiling spirit, softened to fingers, nothing was added but more pain to the child's tortured flesh. Then, detangling in the voice, was a stirring sprout of memory . . . raised eyebrows received and returned with a giggle, spaced teeth, perfect black ripe lips and a sweet of smile from an early morning princess sitting next to an old woman, folding eyebrows like funeral cloth.

"Child of Nana'andisa. We among them who can no walk long in sunlight. They do to me and women others in night what yo' fever keep them long time from do you . . ."

The voice spoke the girl's language brokenly, as one sent with a message to her father from another council. This one though, was like an unwilling messenger, forced to study a new language moments before the time came to speak or face death for not being able to tell.

"This a bad time. Our skin they burn in their name with iron hot before boarding this water craft. On vessel one go bite yu breast, drink yo' little blood. I give self to stop stenchful beast from yu in night, stay toi to yo' side fo' Mother Journey.

"... Speak yu can, can yu speak no?"
". . ."
"If yu speak no, yu die.
"No trees. Days no number.
"So hot days, cold nights, break skin same.
"Demon winds for days whip ship all place.
"Teethful water beasts follow ship.
"Eat the dead, no holy ceremony.
"Who a go forgive who no bury own dead?
"Whoagoforgiveweeeeeeeeeeeeeeeeeeeeeee?
"Aaaaieeeeeeeeeeeeeeeeeeeeeemamaaaaaaaa.
"Whoagoforgivewe?
"Yo' fever stole yu spirit.
"Vie say yu walkin' with death.
"Walkin'dead with no a memory.
"Now so long times since morning.
"Yu call name.
"Nana'andisa!Nana'andisa!"

Then impatiently, as if tired of repeating a message so long to oneself that the actual telling exhausted the very air of breath: "Now. Time. Speak! . . . Then I live . . . fo' nothing . . . then to die I a go . . ."

"Water something is coming out of me, and it is hot and my father's mother my Mama and aunts and sisters . . . and I . . . I do not know what it is . . ." raced the trembling voiceling, choking in wonder and fright, hands balled in fists, elbows clutching to a body of shivers.

"You seeing time, first time . . . woman.

"That what yu being.

"I

"now

"for yu

"mother

"aunt

"sister . . ." said the voice, bodiless, searching for its own comfort, reason, being, sense of purpose, cleansing, passage home.

The woman that was becoming, was losing more of the memory of her last morning encircled by life's rhythm upon the river craft.

Her mother's voice came calling from her day-before. It rose brilliantly clear, rounded as her wifely hips—showing off as a youngest wife could—rose above all the fears, swears, and tears, all vexing, all commands, all renting of language, all stench and prayers, all the maddening laughter, all the dying and defiance, and the visitation of this evil that had stopped the child's rhythm of life in God's Land among His Chosen.

The mother's shepherd call came on top of a heavy pulling of iron and wood away from wood. A hole was sucked open from atop, and drilled through the fetid rotting of humanity. A caravan of light and a howling of leering laughter flooded in, and pressed heavily onto the searing of her skin and dunked in the rapacious pain familiarizing within her body, without consent, without quarter.

The salted temper of air came this time as a destined burden, and again, the light and the laughter crushed the gaping, iron-pressed, fire-branded, wailing souls below. Somewhere a trail of iron was beating loose with haste. From above came the rumbling, down past the craft's outside into a watery gullet of silence.

Her bleeding was squeezing loose through the rag knotted around her waist and between her thighs, seeping silently into a wood-bottom pond. Oh, would it drown her and stifle the cursing below, she wondered. Oh, would it all run out then and swamp the gurgling of curses? Oh, would it be more than the sea and let men and all see her cleansing? Inside, something was wringing loose, and more of something was choking her where the cloth sopped like a fist at the mouth of her womanhood.

"Ship stop. Beasts, dem comin," drilled the spitfire voice of she who was princess neck and pride dancer another world ago.

The bleeding young woman's eyes reeled, burdened, bitingly. A salting poked through her noseholes, as if to petrify her senses.

Her mother's voice, so womanishly free, human, becoming ever more patchy but unrelenting: "Were you a wife . . . a woman . . . adorned with jewels of gold . . . on this journey . . . It is as well . . . let the world know you are a child . . . our children can go far into any country . . . with means of their own . . .

"Come come come child of mine . . . Have you forgotten your name already? . . . Are you deaf to your own mother's voice?

"Nana Mandisa will not wait on you forever you know.

"Come and prepare yourself for a washing and a long journey."

The wake

When Ademus came home, after wading for France through World War One's blood-swamped fields of gnawed-open flesh and bone-gorged trenches, Cyus saw him heading up to Cul-de-Sac where he was the prince of his family.

Cyus, the mannish child of Froston and Selanie Flanders, spied the mounted soldier, and, to this day, he would swear amidst a choking screen of smoke coughed from his Havana gold that "that was the handsomest colored man Oi ever saw."

It was a late sunny afternoon. Seven-year-old Cyus was standing high among the tamarind leaves which were fanning his bare back and imprinting a tattoo of sunlight and shadow on his narrow, freshly sculptured face. The horse-borne figure trotted in respectful silence past the path which opened to Freetown.

A ghost of dust spiraled like a wave of wonder around the stallion as the soldier trotted past the tree-shrouded gateway of Rambaud. The horseman cast a hesitant glance into the village, as if his ears had suddenly begun to ring from someone calling his name. Cyus's head, bowed over the passage of this lone pageant, eyes peeping down through a green-leafed screen of branches, raised at the sudden flight of wind from the east as the war-wounded soldier's stumbling glance returned to a forward gaze.

Cyus felt like the cavalier was looming through the tamarind tree, brushing through the caress of afternoon air. Clouds tumbled for a little while over the settling brilliance of sun.

When the boy caught himself, he was looking at the man's khaki-shirted shoulders, even like the horizon, bearing a sturdy head fastened like a laurel. The sagittarian figure descended with a gentle rocking into the gut, northward.

Through the savanna the soldier rode, singing a guttural hymn no louder than the black steed's hooves pounding like pestles on the grainy dirt road. The trotting silhouette eased through the sleepy fishing village of Grand Case.

The sea-sprayed Cul-de-Sac breeze reached the rider. It lulled him awake from screaming memories of brimstone farted from marauding bombers, veils of fire torching through strange cities, and the scorched lungs of Pelagiel's first born who laid somewhere next to him, punctured, twisted, stitched in a petrified landscape of blooded rags and frost-biting winter.

The horse bristled, bobbed its head, flared its spotted moist nostrils, and pointed its head at La Barrière, the gateway into Cul-de-Sac. Night was soon to fall. The centaur picked its way past the narrow path flanked by rock walls, and galloped into the yard of Sweet Ma.

"O Sweet Mother of God in Heaven, thank yo' for deliverin' my son from the pit of hell an' bringin' him home to us safe and sound," wailed the soldier's mother when she spotted him.

She rose from her dawn-to-dusk watch on the small porch, one hand flung high in praise, the other hurrying her along to keep up with the pointed lead of her cane. The rocking chair, eased of her vigil, flung back and forth, palpitating at the door, rousing the household, echoing throughout the village.

The old woman fell to her knees in the center of the yard, hands and walking stick raised like a tribute before the looming shadow of man and beast etched in twilight. The man braced the horse. The beast neighed and reared on its hind legs away from Sweet Ma, her hands clasped in an ecstasy of prayer. Ademus drew the reigns, commanded silence. He climbed from the horse, which was bowing its head in nervous frenzy.

A burst of kerosene lanterns, bajan and gas lamps encircled the yard, pushing the rim of dusk further into night, casting a halo around the wordless son, his arms now lowered like wings around the old queen, raising Sweet Ma to her trembling feet, wiping her silent tears with his cheeks, embracing her so gently. She twisted her arms around him, warmed the lingering chill festering his bosom. He closed his eyes and purged his soldier's soul. He was home.

Not long after the homecoming, and still at the precipice of his late teens, Ademus plunged the sea again. He landed in Cuba the day *The Havana Post* reported, in one of its multiple columns marching across the front page, that "WAR WAS STILL A POSSIBILITY." The new armistice terms were being put to Germany by Marshal Foch.

The veteran coldly clipped open the paper: Havana's railway unions were boiling over whether to strike. He rolled and holstered the paper under his left arm, picked up his valise from the sidewalk and walked on to find labor and lodging.

For a few months, he cut cane in the sugar fields of the island's south central region. Next, he headed for the southeastern city of Santiago de Cuba where he took up the carpenter's trade. Then he went to the States and labored in the dockyards of New York City.

The year the stock market crashed, scattering another tower of Babel, cracking the nerves of big men, shoving them from their high office windows to walled streets and, in the process, dropping their weighted dealings like brimstone on the raw backs of the world's poor, Ademus sailed south to work the docks of Curaçao. Not long after, he went over to Aruba where, armed with a machinist certificate from the States, he quickly found work in Lago's oil refinery, and on Saturdays and Sundays did a little woodworking in The Village.

"So you see, Pearl, Pappie was all over the world, and he put roof over a lot ah Windward Islanders' heads in Aruba," recalled Ademus's oldest daughter, Hennee.

"A lot ah S'maatiners and all had to sleep

under cardboard boxes when they first went to Aruba. Some ah we sittin' down right here this afternoon had to endure that." The older women of the family's villages nodded their assent. Hennee's daughter, Pearl, sat relishing the recounting and competition of stories. This was the customary threading of genealogy, which had started in the kitchen in the late afternoon among kinswomen and guests who came to pay their last respects.

"We had pride. We build up we self, yes. But a lot doan like to talk about the wounds we got all where we went. Some got shame because ah that, and swear how they was never goin' back S'maatin becausin ain nothing there, an' ain nothing goin' come there.

"They use to call S'maatin 'The Rock' an' not everybody meant it in a good way. Some ah dem use to call S'maatin Sing Sing. That was the name of a bad prison in the States. It use to hurt my heart to hear how some ah we oan people use to badtalk this sweet little land when in Aruba some ah us get treated so bad.

"Now yo' does see a lot ah dem same people back in S'maatin trying to make it after Aruba spit them out, refusin' their children born there scholarships or a home so sweet like S'maatin.

"Some still foolin' deyself. But S'maatin always take her own in, is just that some ah dem doan know how to come home without feeling they have to prove they 'Rubians or Kurosoleneans or wherever else on God earth they make."

Hennee was one who had been taken in early by the lush rock of earth. When they were in Aruba, Ademus and her mother spoke not a day, and not always to each other, without blessing their homeland.

In her late teens, the St. Martin woman who came to be Ademus's wife had visited Dahta every Saturday. From the trader's wares she selected with a housewife's pickiness a parcel of fish and sometimes provision imported from Rambaud—all to be paid for at month's end. She also carried home to her mother, father, and youngest brother, the latest Village melee, and news from "Home."

"Oi never see a young man wuk so quiet in all meh life. An he carry heself so old; like he see all what the world got to suffer. Buh wha' a gentleman!" Dahta had confided in her.

"Oh," clipped the wife-to-be, stumbling a glance the carpenter's way. Just then the wind that bends the boughs of the Divi Divi tree cooled the sweat blushing down Ademus's brow. He threw his head up heavily, sprinkling perspiration back at the twist of sawdust fanning toward his eyes. All he had to do now was hinge the door for Dahta and his job was done.

When he had finished rubbing his always so red eyes, he opened them to catch the fresh, cattish-sculptured features turning away.

The breeze bearing the sting of his sweat pursued the young woman. She felt the breath of his desire caress her floral skirt nervously to the slender crescent calves of her legs. His heart pounded with the drive of a hammer soaking a nail through a zinc roof.

You old fool, he had thought dryly to himself, it is time you settle down and raise a family.

One year later, the two took vows of matrimony. Months after, Hennee was born. The little family moved from its huddled quarters in The Village to Rooi Congo. The June bride would clean no more house for the American chieftains of Lago because Ademus doubled his side jobs to provide for his wife and child with the same tenacity of duty and manly pride as he had been doing for his kindred in Sweet Ma's house.

The handsome prince did not pry long at the tough shyness of his exceedingly beautiful wife.

Her way was sweetly bewitching. It was as if she was never sure it was him when they had been making love. Then a wild flutter in her would subside, and recognizing the breath of his desire, how well he held her, she would become softly reserved and embrace him with a far-off sigh. This was like an eternal courtship to him. She would open up in her time, he reasoned. His wife cooked, washed, managed the household with great and meticulous care, and bore Ademus eight children. At the age of five, and upon the birth of the third child, Hennee had been sent to St. Martin to live with Sweet Ma.

"My father's heart was always in S'maatin," recalled Hennee while looking proudly at her daughter. Hennee stretched her neck and looked into the breeze of the late afternoon easing through the kitchen window. She raised a single eyebrow starkly high like her mother's when offended by bad table manners, "And your grandmother was always talking about Rambaud like God self make his throne there. So whenever I hear them talking about sending me to Sweet Ma, I would get so excited that all I could do was dream about goin' to this blessed S'maatin."

As she spoke, the wharf where the Antillia had docked came to mind. The ship had waved at passengers to hurry aboard. Her mother, with a hurricane's suddenness, had wrenched her suitcase from her clutching hand, grappled her by the shoulders and almost kneeling before her, muttered, beseeched the petite traveler not to get familiar in other people's house, and to keep out of the damned sea.

"The day I left for S'maatin must be when my troubles started with my mother. The first time she lay hands on me was when we were waiting to board the Antillia. I intend to ask her why she got cold and rough like a man that day.

"But as for Sweet Ma, Pearl, my choil, what a loving old woman yo' great grandmother was. Hmm, hmm, hmm." Hennee settled back into her chair, her gaze lost in the distance, her mind adrift . . .

Upon The Rock "Hennee blossomed into such a noice choil," Sweet Ma had always said before she passed away. Hennee became the princess of the three villages which had encompassed her mother's and father's people for over one hundred and fifty years.

At the age of thirteen, Hennee had been called back to Aruba where she tended house for a mother she did not recognize. There she was instructed, by the same voice that warned her at the wharf, to get up every foreday morning to cook Ademus's food, and to mind the other children. The only thing the daughter was not charged to lay hands on was the wondrous bread her mother started baking and selling to make ends meet during the Second World War.

Once while washing the breakfast dishes, Hennee had asked when she would start going to school with her brothers and sisters. Ademus's wife answered the pretty girl's back with a severe thump. One fore-day morning, the daughter fell asleep by the busy stove, against the wall by the kitchen window. Her dozing hand eased from the cooking spoon which slipped into the heavy cast-iron pot of oxtail and pea soup. A long sprinkle of liquid clambered over the pot's rim and pinched the sleeping beauty awake. Before she could somehow intercept the smell of burning food from penetrating her mother's white mosquito net, Hennee had been visited by a rain of meps and knuckles all upside her head. Hot food, lunch box, the tray of dried dishes, and a hand-flaying Hennee flew to the floor of rust-colored tiles.

"That will teach you, you lazy little wench, not to sleep in my kitchen! The rice should ah bun yo' too! And how much toime Oi keep telling yo' to put 'way the dishes when yo' wash them up at night!" bellowed the woman, hands akimbo, a spit of foam lurking at the corner creases of her mouth.

Ademus appeared, half of his face still pasted with shaving cream, bare-backed and in his boxer shorts, while his wife hovered with the menacing grace of a vulture over the curled-up child. He positioned himself in the midst of the assault. His daughter ducked and hid under her father's presence. He just stood there, hands raised in front of him like someone was pointing a gun at his heart.

The mother held her tightly fisted hands up. She raged in a torturous babble, "Yo' think yo' get away from it? I could drown yo' with blows here today. Yo' can't get away from it!" She flung herself out of the kitchen like a blind gale, reached the toilet and had to sit on the big potty to catch herself. Ademus ate no breakfast that morning, took no lunch to work that day.

When he returned home he brought sugar-cakes for his children, and as usual, doted over them all. He enthroned Hennee on his knee, kissing her bruised left eye. And when the other children skipped away, he told her war stories, tales of cane-cutters, and the milder dockyard jokes. Together they conjured up Sweet Ma and St. Martin like a game of slapping-pinchers.

In the early evening, the pair shared fables of jumbies and Brer Rabbit passed on to them by Sweet Ma on nights when the full moon worshiped sloping hills and caressed ponds, lagoon, and flatlands with amorous, longing delight.

The night following the attack on his sister, Ademus's first son awoke on the floor in a cold-sweat. He had been pushed from the bed, clutching his covers, by blood-curdling howls from his father's flashback. War cries gutted the house: "They-coming-from-the-east!-They-coming-from-the-east!" The nightmares had returned with vengeance to haunt the old soldier. Ademus longed for home.

When Hennee had left to live with Sweet Ma, the tough shyness of his wife—who was filled with child—had begun to swell, as if from an inward poison. Ademus had shielded himself in silence, and to him was born a second son. With his first daughter now back in the house, his wife's inward poison became a pus-smooth boil-head. Yet, to him, barring he did not linger too long at the chasm of her piercing gaze when she berated him for one nit-picking thing or other, her sweet beauty of form and face endured with a freshness.

Ademus was nevertheless aware of the web of division the wife was attempting to weave between him and their offspring. She courted their attention jealously, punished disloyalty, and scorned his fatherly gifts of sweets that the children so thrilled in receiving.

Through the louvers, his wife would witness the delicate ritual of the father's rough, oil-stained hands breaking sugarcakes like a pelican's beak, imparting into soft cupped palms morsels of grated, boiled, and baked sugar, cinnamon, and coconut. When the children skipped away in a joyous rite nearing pandemonium, her triumphant smile at their rapid dispersal would be scalded by the bonding circle father and first daughter drew around each other. It was an aurora that bewitched the wife and caused her to recoil into a bitter, unexplainable labor of vengeful plots.

In the late nineteen fifties, Ademus retired on Lago's pension and brought his family home to St. Martin. He had been sending money since he first started to work in Aruba. Trusted Cousin Nico received the money and supervised the building of the dream house on Ademus's late father's succession land in Cole Bay.

The Lago and veteran's pensions, combined with the sums from his on-going carpentry work, provided enough funds for Ademus to finish building a nice little four-bedroom dwelling for his family.

"Ven Jull dem put on that last coat ah paint, giol, Oi felt like a new bride moving in," his wife once told next-door neighbor, Terez.

The paint's smell had chased her and their daughters to her late father and mother's house in Rambaud. Ademus took the last two boys by Sweet Ma. There he taught his sons to fish and hunt crabs by kerosene lantern at night.

The family held out for nine grateful but anxious nights. The first night back in the house, with the smell of paint still trying to stifle everybody like they were in a tomb, the old wife told her husband that she would not have him.

"Get it in yo' head now. The last bedroom by the kitchen is where yu goin' sleep." This she punctuated with a stabbing finger in the direction of the bedroom and a sawing glare which cauterized his heart.

He passed through one set of children's bedrooms. The boys were spread out in sleep. Ademus found his cot made up well and proper in the last bedroom. There he slept since. There the cries of battle rolled off his tongue nightly like lunging brigades of thunder.

The wife had not one day let up in her household management. With her husband's money and the *sous-sous* from her baking, she suited out a comfortable castle. Ademus's handsome matching cedar bed, night table, and what he thought of as his reading chair, she ordered through Yanki's store not long after his banishment from the conjugal chamber.

A few years after coming home to St. Martin, all of their children escaped abroad to work or study. Then Hennee's five-year-old Pearl arrived from Aruba for a visit. Latched in her right hand was the wrist of the first son of Ademus's second son. The grandparents received their grandchildren with a certain relief. It was a particular prayer of their graying years that they thought might not have come true. Ademus doted over his first grandchildren like a benign god.

Hennee's Pearl, now a pre-law student at Columbia University, gleefully interrupted her mother's reverie of time and things gone by with a topping of her own wonder years: dressed-up Sunday afternoon walks and cool Saturday morning strolls to Simpson Bay Beach with her "Gran Adey."

As children, they would run and romp in the sand as children do, wash in the shallow, crystal clear water, collect shells, pick sea grapes and salt them in the sea before eating them from cones of sea grape leaves. After Ademus returned from his long laps against the troops of ocean waves, he would play catch with the children as much as an old soldier could before slipping into a feet-dredged trench of sand.

His grandchildren would trap him by raising sand castles over the length of his body as the guttural hymns from his breast soothed him asleep. The little ones would cuddle their salt-seasoned and sand-powdered cheeks next to his, one child on each side, and fall asleep too.

The grandmother always cursed up a storm when the excited voices told her how "Gran Adey went out so far in the sea. Then he duck ondah de water and we get so skiod."

"Not me," injected the first born of Ademus's second son. "Gran Adey is the bes' swimmer in the whole wohl." The boy's father had sworn to his elder brother before boarding a Scandinavian whaler at the rambling age of seventeen that no woman would live long enough to treat him the way he saw his mother treat his father.

"Yeah, boy!" glowed Hennee's child. At this point there would be a feeble silence. The grandmother's love would start to backslide. A demon of thought would split her into a double sourness she now realized she could not control.

She would think how the little pup looked just like blasted Hennee and Sweet Ma. Then she would hear the ocean's waves boiling like a geyser and see her older sister, Saysa, right in front of her. The fright of the last secret specter always filled her with a foreboding of deep loss and wrenching guilt. She would have to sit down and catch her breath.

"Yeah, boy, then Gran Adey come up outta de water and swim to us just like a fish. We staat to run and laugh 'till he ketch us ondah de grape tree."

The beach tale usually ended with them telling how they fell asleep. Grandmother would coarsen her voice and curse "that doting man" who "doan know the chil'ren could ketch a draft and ketch their death ah cold."

At this time, no matter where he was in the house or about the yard, the Gran Adey would summon a trampling voice and call to Hennee's daughter. With the infant fawn's ignorance of a hunter's pursuing glare, the girl would skip in mindless sing-song to her grandfather. The boy bounced behind her, his hands outstretched, lips pursed, airplane sounds roaring.

"Doan think yu' goin' get away without washing off that sea salt and sand before ahl yo' eat!" exhaled the grandmother.

The wife still cooked with a sweetness which made many people forget table manners and, with closed eyes, swoon over their fingers. She arranged Ademus's solitary meals in an old, beat-up, small tin pot. The aroma of her blameless kitchen would shatter when she slopped the food in front of him as if she were feeding the hogs penned in the Heyligers' backyard.

Yet he savored his meals with the grand appetite of a banqueting king. Ademus was banned from eating at the dining table too, then from walking through the castle's glass-cased shrine of a living room.

When company came, and the wife never ceased drawing people to her—even after cursing them for something or the other—Ademus would sit in the backyard under the shade of banana trees she had planted not far from the outdoor toilet and bath. There, when his sight was better, he would read *Windward Islands Opinion* and the Lago newspaper mailed to him from the company.

Whenever evening called, he would ease into his rocking chair on the porch, his grandchildren encircling his feet like kittens, listening and not listening, crawling under the chair, playing last-lick, giggling, as he imparted tall tales of Brer Rabbit and Compa Nansi. Sometimes he read news from afar to the wide-eyed bundles of giggling glee.

The wife took the grandchildren to church in Marigot every Sunday and cursed her husband "for always story-telling and never once reading the chil'ren any Bible stories." Ademus was glad to read the newspapers to his grandchildren. He had always wanted to do that for his children too, but never got around to it.

"Ahl yu' list'ning, chil'ren?"

"Yes, Gran Adey!" they would say in melodious union, jumping to attention at his side, hugging him, kissing and stroking his gray gruffly-bearded cheeks, lumbering up to play see-saw on his tired old knees.

Sweet Ma knew of her son's painful life journey. Some say it grieved her to death. She never visited Ademus's house. Upon his regular visits, sometimes with grandchildren slinging themselves from his hands like tail-wagging puppies, he was welcomed into the matriarch's home by kindred old and young.

A table was laid before him of their succession land's finest fruits and provision, meat from the thinning stock of his late father's cattle which were once fatted in pastures for trade to St. Barths and Guadeloupe, and yard-oven-baked bread dabbed with butter churned from soured milk by Sweet Ma's own hands. Sweet drinks of lime or soursop or tamarind softened the thirst of all and rounded full out the bellies of the children.

Ademus searched his aged mother's eyes and witnessed every parting of her lips, hoping, listening, for some kind of explanation about his wife's behavior. Sweet Ma never spoke bad or good about the woman her son brought into her family by marriage.

"After his mother passed away, Ademus lived only for his grandchildren. The rest of the world 'round him disappeared. That man nearly never utter a word to a mortal soul since," said Cyus to the men who had come by night to the old soldier's wake. They sat together on the porch, shook their heads slowly, and camped on a trail of memories of the man whose coffin lay closed in the glass-cased shrine of a living room.

"Oi first saw Ademus the day he come home from the first war. I was a little boy and didn't even know he was meh uncle. Through him meh faader got to go Aruba, find wuk, and later sen' fo' vie."

"But Cyus, if a man alive knows, it must be you. Tell us, woi that woman of a wife treat Ademus so bad?" asked the bending tower of an elder called Raddie.

"Raddie, meh boy, let me tell ahl yo', becausin like you say, if there wuz ever a man 'live to know, it must be me. And as God is my witness, this is wha' Oi know."

The men fitted their ears to the preamble of what they were certain would be a yarn of which even their wives knew little.

"Cyus, how much could you know what husband ni wife never tell their bestest friend?" came a grouching voice.

"Doodey, you blasted old doubting Thomas, doan humbug meh luck here now," reared Cyus, shifting his weight in the easy chair from which Ademus had longed for womankind's comfort.

"Let the man speak nah, Doodey," came an ominous grumble from nervous-voiced Joaba, prodigal son of Samuel, Cyus's late brother.

Cyus turned to his nephew seated on the

steps leading to the porch. "Go inside," he cranked, "tell your mother to ask the widow to send us more rum and brandy. The night is chilly. Vie throat is hoarse an' truth goin' give birth tonight."

The prodigal son was a terse and coarse man of the sea. As a mere boy, he had sailed on a steamer to chalk India, long before Indians even dreamed of St. Martin. He had unfolded a tale before Cyus some years ago, uncurled it like Shiva's necklace of skulls, confided it in a terror-struck voice which scurried away his stammering. In it the beggars of Calcutta thronged and squatted in a ghastly procession which still haunts the old storyteller, crawls his blood. It festered in him a gnawing disgust of his nephew for impaling him with what he thought of as a leprous vision of man's fall from grace.

With the doubting Doodey silenced and the promise of liquor to warm the spirits, the cloister of men eased back in their seats with a vow to silence.

"Gentlemen, they say when a man lowe too much it is that woman who goin' betray him. Oi doan know if it is so 'causin Oi lowe a whole lot, but that woman of moine is an angel sen' straight from The Holy Father.

"Buh Ademus was a victim, as they say nowadays, of circumstance. Oi wasn't there buh Oi heard it from the mango seller Wappa, from she mouth self. She got it from Inez boy who used to teach Sunday school in Kura Kabai. They say that ven Ademus—he must ah been thirty—lay eyes on the child that was to be his wife, he was struck by a bolt of lightening!"

"Hmmmmm," the men thundered from far distances within. Some nodded their whitening heads slowly. Some stroked their sagging thighs, stretched a cobweb of cracks from their back, scratched the gray stubble coating their necks.

A few passed their fingers over their mouths and squeezed their noble chins. One grinned irrepressibly. One looked up at the half-lighted flesh of moon painting a path for the heavy cloud-covered night, and whispered something. His compadre smiled sinfully. Next to him a blind one bowed sheepishly and tapped his knobby cane stubbornly. Another pressed his fingers to his brow. This one dragged his head back with a slow soundless laughter. That one clapped the arching back of his partner. The partner rocked back and forth like a centennial sandbox tree trunk shoved by a wandering heft of wind.

Such a wordless commotion was spawned that Cyus had to raise his hands like a preacher. They all quietened into that commanding seated silence of old Black men.

"Ahl yo' know, it is lowe vie talking 'bout. There is the lowe all ah us know. And there is the lowe that knows only some ah us.

"Raddie, Ademus didn't had a bad wife. No, she wasn't a bad woman either. Oi cahn tell ahl yo' she treated that man badder than any of you been treated some time or the other. Truth is simple as a babe born in a manger on Christmas mahnin'. She just didn't lowe that man.

"I think she find it out ven Hennee was born. Come to her mind like Hennee had to belong to she and another. It's no secret how she 'buse that choil. I self rescue meh dear family a couple ah times from the blows. An' it me she stay by in Aruba after Ademus dem come back S'maatin."

The old men, almost in unison, paused tensely. They drained the last of the wet spirits from their glasses.

"Boys, the widow Edonia loved another. There wasn't much people in S'maatin those days. The Baroque dem boy—dey was a mulatto family, gone now, die out from in-mixing bad blood since slavery toime, think they white—he fall for young Edonia.

"He mother sen' him away becausin dey'ain wahn mix with Black people. Meh mother tell me they toi him up like a young bull, and he uncle from St. Barths took him off to sea bawling till blood come out he mouth, nose, an' oize. Meh mother say, like the girl wasn't good in she head after that."

"Buh, Cyus, the widow is fair skin," queried a sun-reddened Grand Case descendant of saltpickers.

"Buh not all she people," coughed Cyus. "She family Black. Like most ah us, make up with all them complexions.

"Mr. Baroque cuss the faader an' mother stink becausin they oan son come from Marigot to Rambaud serenading the girl. I wuz their neighbor and see that cussing with moi own little oize looking down from a Jamaica plum tree. Yes, she was a beauty, as you can still see, till she up in years.

"They say only she older sister, Saysa, jet black, was more beautiful. She die before I born. Buh Oi think ahl yo old enough to know that she disappeared. People say in the sea.

"No sirree. The widow Edonia just didn't

treat my uncle Ademus like a woman should treat her man. But not a man alive can stan' up here tonight and say she didn't do a lot ah what a wife should do for a husband. None ah ahl yo' could look Cyus Augustinus Flanders in he face an' tell him that the widow didn't nurse all she chil'ren."

"For God's sake, Cyus, talk sense, man. Wife, husband, man, woman, what is the difference?" asked a man who wandered up to the porch, his frame leaning on a cane which he did not seem to need.

"Shut up, Camille, or go back home!" pitched Calix, a disturbingly thin, hoarse-voiced Simpson Bay fellow.

"Man, woman, husband, wife are the same and not the same," explained Cyus calmly.

"Every man must come to know and understand who he is and all the parts he made from. A man is made up ah many parts—a husband, the work he do, the children he father, a lover, a jokey fellow, the good he do, the bad he let happen, a warrior for justice, a rogue, a friend, the shame he had to do which nobody but he still know."

A cut of lightning gaped from the cloud-troubled sky. Like a pig shifting its weight from slumber to drunken wake, Viol grunted a response to the hurled bolt of thunder. He had dozed off in the corner right under the widow's bedroom window.

The others looked at him. Another incendiary flash prosecuted his rum-mocked body and drooling features.

"There is the man who carry a fear fo' life," continued Cyus. "There is the coonoomoonoo full ah horns, a *crapo la* full ah it, a *gallo hiero* full ah spurs. These are some of the parts making up a man. The better man foind he parts, bring them together and live in peace with heself."

"Peace?" gargled Viol, his hair, refusing to gray or thin, still slicked back and greasily wet after seventy years.

"No man can find peace with a woman," he pronounced, his feet tapping like angry bat wings.

"Speak your own mind, Viol. What is in your house is your business. We all got a story. When we are no longer here it another man to tell it, da's if we lucky. Leh me tell Ademus's story in peace," said Cyus. Some of the men laughed wickedly.

Pearl appeared with a new regiment of glasses crowded on a narrow silver tray. Ademus's first grandson bounced behind, cradling a bottle of Miss Ruby's fine home-made guavaberry in one hand, and in the other hand, hoisting other drinks between a rack of fingers. Hennee followed with a steaming pot of souse. Joaba brought an assortment of bowls, pepper-sauce, and a fist of spoons.

"Accept our sympathies, Miss Hennee," said one.

"Welcome home, Miss Hennee," said others in a domino factor of humble utterances.

"The States agree w' yu," offered another.

The older men from her father's and mother's villages moved to their feet. Some removed their caps and hats. Others placed their hands to their hearts as they called her name. There was a gray-bearded one who did not stand, but bowed like an old lion, the wood of the old cedar chair pressing out a sound of uncommon weight. He was laying eyes on the spitting grace of her mother, and he was pleased.

Hennee's daughter, who had joined her mother in New York after the years in Aruba and St. Martin, moved assuredly among the ancient male keepers of the wake, serving them in honored silence, parting her smile when spoken to in a whisper of "You're welcome," and

"Thank you."

This mane of old St. Martin ate and drank and made merriment. Negus and his brothers strummed their guitars and sang the poetry of San Pedro de Macoris, defying death to be proud of the sleep it casts over each of life's kind. Luke Baly rattled the old frames with quimbés everyone thought had been forgotten in the hills of Freetown and lost in the fertile valleys of Colombier.

"Yes!" exclaimed Cyus, raising his rum glass for a toast, "Leh me go on nah, gentlemen."

"We didn't forget you!" shouted Raddie, placing his empty souse bowl under the stool with a scrape that the widow and Hennee were bound to raise an eyebrow and fret over the next day.

Viol's glass trembled out of his rickety grip as he was about to meet Cyus's toast. Fangs of lightning jagged through the night. Viol blinked from the quick blinding grin of light. The glass fell to his lap, jingling with an alarm of ice, staggered over, and peed the rum out.

"No!" he cursed as the pungent stain soaked through his trousers and molested his shriveled private. He chased the glass from his thighs, but it hugged his right knee with the ice in tow, ducked under his left leg, and rapped the floor with a mute force.

"Uh huh," frowned the prodigal.

"Ademus want a drink!" decreed Negus, dripping a few sips of Miss Ruby's fine guavaberry in the center of their grounding.

Viol waved through a chorus of thigh-slapping laughter and in earshot of Hennee grunted, "Damn it! Bring me another drink, somebody, meh mouth dry like a frigid hen hole!"

"Hear liquor talking?" signaled Raddie.

There was a rougher round of laughter that thinned as Hennee and daughter returned bearing each a tray with healthy saucer-borne portions of coconut tart and pound cake, and a drink which Raddie removed and handed casually to Viol.

The women departed. Cyus raised his glass again and cast a crossed eye at Camille, who threw the same eye at Viol who was licking his lips miserably. The others met Cyus's glass in union, but not a word was uttered. The ice floating in glasses chimed to a devout silence.

"What Oi know about lowe is what I learn from life," resumed Cyus.

"Life guide me to a knowledge that learns a man this. Ven one or two defy the destiny of lowe's desire, it is Providence self that scorns them. Drives them out of life's light like Adam and Eve from The Garden. And it lowe self goin' stand up in they throat like an angel with a fiery sword, without mercy, and cut them down like a sickness, like consumption."

"God is love," contradicted Camille, almost out of breath.

"Confound it, man," blasted Cyus at being interrupted. "God is the lowe sacrificed for his children. Then there's that kind ah lowe's desire for its own destiny. It is a wrathful angel of man's heart if that destiny is snuffed out by false pride, rapacious drunkenness, and covetousness.

"That kind ah lowe is the jealous stepchild of God. He self doan know what to do with it. So He sen' it to live in man to tame it in secrecy. But all it does do when it get denied is consume life and all the living in a rampage. Then only death for the dead must be cooling enough to clean the soul of that kind ah pain."

"The Bible says, vengeance is mine sayeth the Lord," came back Camille with feuded charge, raising to his feet and drilling his thin, iron-point cane into a grass-lined crack of cement at the foot of the three steps leading to the porch.

"You still reading too much of that Rosicrucian business, or something else got you talking out your head! Cyus, you think you understand the politics of this world better than its maker?"

Cyus waved him silent. Some of the other men grumbled. Brother Fondie, whose father's youthful late night serenades were still legendary for ripening the delightful favors of Sweet Ma before she married old man Johannus, clapped his hands with the annoyed elegance of a Moorish pasha.

Camille reluctantly found the wisened and tired eyes of the beretted older head, and turned his back on the ancient assembly. He pouted and stared at the angry-looking clouds heaving under the half-naked moon.

"Man must know he is here to labor and lowe. To battle for right and build that which is right. Ademus was a dutiful soldier, a tradesman, a good man, a husband provider, and a loving father to his children and his children's children. What more can a man do?" asked the storyteller.

"Man is a beast of burden," offered the old man of the sea they called Capi.

"Capi, meh son, is you who tek moi faader, an' Mr. Priest sitting over there so quiet tonight, an' all dem so to Sannemengo, to cut cane and what not. When the contract up, or their chil'ren reach the age to come back, you bring 'em back up the oilans, stoppin' here an' there to mek a little trade ah coconuts an' ting, an' leave off dem odah oilan' people in their country.

"Jeezus Chroist, Capi, da's how old yu is. A mule who beat de sea and laugh to God face fo' nevah losin' a mortal soul to that same ocean where dey dump slaves wen they get old and sick like some ah we hereso. Buh man is no beast," raised Emanuel, the joiner from Over-The-Pond, rheumatism sneering in his joints as he spoke.

"Man is the lord of Creation," sparred Brother Fondie. He was the eldest of the gathering. This was the most he had spoken since the wake began hours ago. His words marched out of him with the gravity of lava unchallenged and braced the congregation to a muteness which seemed like reverence.

The oath Fondie just uttered was placed in him by a correct-talking mother who feared neither men nor their gods, but dearly loved one of both. She taught her son that "Black men must study a trade and seek their proper power to match any man if we are ever to be a people."

Until her passing, she kept candles lighted

next to a time-faded picture of Saint Martin de Pores for the safe passage of her only child's father, Joseph. After returning from St. Thomas, preaching of a redemption not far off, he set sail for England at the invitation of T. R. Makonnen, and then on to Liberia to meet up with the visions of Edward Wilmot Blyden and Marcus Garvey. He was never heard from again.

Fondie grew to be well-off, a father of thirty-two children, all of whom he saw educated, a husband to three wives who went on to rest ahead of him. He now lived in what he called a deserved bliss with his once-housekeeper from Dominica. He still lit candles by the saint's picture, flanked by worn photographs of his mother, and the father he never once laid eyes on.

"Yes I," came a soft, unseasoned voice, loosening the hold of age.

Lord Fondie smiled cautiously and weighed his head in the direction of the young woman who had answered him. Her crown of locks, a luminous copper headdress under the halfmoon, rained down her breasts as she beamed over Cyus's head to sight the source of wisdom. She spied Fondie with a smile so much like his own that it troubled his eyes.

When he focused through his black horn-rimmed spectacles, his slightly trembling right hand raised his beret to her. It was Sheba, daughter of his last child by live-in companion. She winked at her grandfather in whose books she excavated the royal name by which every one now calls her. She swung her legs, clawed the cement ledge on which she was sitting, and pushed her shoulders above the horizon of her chin. She was hungry for Cyus's testament and revelation to chant forward.

The storyteller twisted his aged self around to see who had spoken, and he met a curtain of young faces, reflecting a mosaic of family and friends.

He looked eastward, before him, and that part of the verandah's cement ledge had sprouted a mangrove of children in whose faces he saw faces of his youth.

He looked to the front door which Ademus had not been permitted by his wife to walk through. It was wide open and choking with the issue of Sweet Ma's line. A cricket hailed out, and the griot glanced northward, to where smaller, wide-eyed children were cropped on the welcome mat, enthralled at the porch's entrance.

In some of the little faces were etched features of the new blood which was coursing in the land . . . and they were all beautiful.

Behind them he recognized his sons, "always late," he thought. He still swears he does not know how one had become a doctor and the other a guesthouse owner. Their pride surged to greet him, and he saluted with a dreamy nod. The brothers leaned closer together.

Cyus's eyes locked with those of Camille, who was now seated in a chair on the pavement, directly behind the wide-eyed bunch of children. Camille was holding to his bosom grandnephew David. It was the son of his last sister's third child. Only Camille forgave this niece for bearing a child at seventeen for one who refused, still, to claim his manhood. She lived in her uncle's house and tonight stood at his back in a casino worker's uniform, the porch light twisting her mouth into a ravenous mask of curiosity, her hands resting like a velvet coal saşh around her beloved "*Oom* Cam."

The eyes of Cyus and Camille wrestled in vain to seek some overdue rapprochement.

They once laughed and cursed and vexed and fought each other, and for each other. Where you saw one, you were bound to see the other: in school, pitching marbles, flying kites, trapping mountain doves, lassoing lizards, chasing girls; through church sermons, cricket, cockfights, bullfight dances, PMIA and lodge meetings. During elections and at the domino table, it was always them against the world. In their labor-driven days abroad they fisted bigger men than themselves who called them disdainfully *"nègre anglais"* in Guadeloupe and *"ingles stinkie"* in Aruba and Curaçao. Back in St. Martin, they had to fight for each other to get scholarships or a piece of government land for their children.

Then Camille's name was slapped without his permission on the election list of the ruling party. That party's bossman became Cyus's sworn enemy. For Cyus dared to call him to his face, with the whole world looking, a thief and a liar for hijacking Camille's good name. The politician took back Cyus's son's scholarship to study medicine.

The party boss had also threatened to recall the scholarships of two of Camille's nine children—the first of his family to go to college in the two hundred years that he knew his people's navel string to be buried in the Sweet Land.

Camille got sixty-three votes and split his family in half during that election. Cyus, never told of the threat, accused Camille of cowardice for not fighting back like a man. The two parted ways and bittered over their friendship with venomous wrought.

Now after nearly twenty years, Camille shook his silver-fleeced head as if to say, "Yes, Cy, we all right."

The storyteller drew a meticulously creased white handkerchief from the back pocket of his khaki pants and waved it open, blew his nostrils severely, and dabbed his eyes with trembling swiftness.

He composed himself in the rocking chair. There was a gaping hush as he folded the handkerchief along its old linen lines and stuffed it in the same shirt pocket from which he freed one of two Havana golds. He inhaled the legend of tobacco rolled between purple thighs, sent the cigar to his altar of lips, twisted its tip to a black wetness which glistened as he pulled it from his mouth, and guided it back in.

Joaba, the prodigal, was there to set the fire. As Cyus drew on the tobacco, the air polished the lighted tip with embers of silence. He exhaled. A tangled battalion of smoke pushed from the storyteller's mouth and nose, ambushing his hands and raiding the prodigal's senses. A communion of smoke-knotted air plaited into the locks and lungs of Sheba. The youngsters next to her fanned briskly as they tried to stifle cough and funny faces. The precious bundles on the floor giggled and threw their bodies into each other with glee.

"Capi, Emanuel, Brother Fondie," returned Cyus with added eloquence. He paused. "Camille." The congregation accepted the reconciliation.

"God is great," whispered Raddie. He had never ceased trying to get Cy and Cam to "just talk out the problem."

"All of you is right. Vie is of a race older than time, and mightier than time remembers. But vie begin in this land as beasts of burden. Beasts of the fields. Coffle for evil men."

"True," cooed the soft dove voice from behind.

"We began in the mud, as all men does do. From burden we come. But by God and the might that is in every man to study hard and wuk the grounds he stan' on, vie must rise on we oan as a people, or vie goin' perish in the backside of humiliation. Yessah, vie must be lords in this Creation. Not in the other world. Oi mean roight here in this sweet land vie all call home."

A soul-echoing wail rushed from inside the house, chasing frantically on the tail of wood shutting in a final thud on top of another board.

Johannus, the only-born of Calvin, Ademus's second son, rose from where he was transfixed on one knee at his father's side, climbed between the mangrove of children, jumped to the ground, and as his sun-rusted locks lashed the peace of night, stretched out his hands, pursed his lips, and raged along the side of the house to the kitchen door.

The storyteller lowered his head, lips parted. The smaller children looked around wildly and tucked into each other with muffled sounds. Calvin looked at his elder brother. Both sighed. Camille made the sign of the cross, then passed his palm over David's forehead, eyes, nose, and mouth. Fondie tipped his felt cap.

The prodigal rose to his feet, facing Cyus with the haunting memory they shared. He stood, stiff, like a sentinel burdened to know the hour of each passing.

"Gone over to Zion to prepare a place," prayed the be-locked dove.

Mother Nez, who in earlier times administered the formula of the dead before Long Gun returned home and opened a funeral home, had just closed the coffin. It was nearing midnight. Most of the women, in a convent of their own stories, had a clear view of the anointing and closing ritual. Hennee's daughter, filled to the brim with an afternoon-to-night of Sweet Ma and other stories, was among them.

The granddaughter rushed forward with a maddening cry, hands reaching before her, gasping for breath, then wordlessly beseeching the old woman of herbal and Ponum secrets, not to close that coffin and open the gate to beyond before she had seen who laid there so still. Not before she had placed her cheek next to the cheek of the body to see for true if it was really her "Gran Adey" who was in there.

The young woman had only last week railed against her professors with that timeless arrogance of youth she and Johannus paraded through the halls of learning. Now, fatigued as if from a *'zépaules* for the very opening and voyage she sought to stall, she fainted over a trunk of weary limbs. The old sisterhood labored to hold her from rolling to the rust-colored tiles.

Johannus appeared in the doorway, his hands grabbing the door's frame like Samson. He lunged for his jewel, his light, his pilot. His fingers shoveled roughly under her body. He pulled his Pearl from the bed of aged knees and stocking-encased thighs. Her weight pulled him back to his knees.

"Don't touch her," he growled, "leave us alone." He clamped his body around Pearl like a soldier's helmet covered with a dreaded net of locks.

Hennee, in the doorway leading to the living room, felt her daughter's fingers leaving her palms to Johannus's claim. She pressed her grieving body down to the chair, longingly turned to face her father's closed coffin, straightened her back, smoothed the hem of her favorite linen dress over her knees.

"Death is not liberation for we, the living," said the storyteller in a nasal tone. He puffed on his Havana gold, coughed, buttoned his shirt to the collar, and shook a sturdy finger at the still standing prodigal son.

"Ahl yu' know we started to tell the story of one man, and all we doing so far is talkin' about the race of people we come from. Who we belong to is we."

The prodigal folded his rough, hairy, muscled hands like two crane hooks crossing, and stood at a marine's watch.

"I am passing it on to you now!" Cyus's hand returned to a fold of relief in his lap.

"Ahl yo' know we sat around here first as men of nearly the same sex. Generations from

Brother Fondie to my Samuel boy here."

The prodigal closed his eyes. He saw visions of his tribe huddled in a phlegm of poverty. Gaunt elders of the tribe battled their emaciated children who were fighting to crawl up moss-green pillars of salt. Red ooze seeped from a blue vat at the pinnacle, hovered miserly and would not wash down. The children were ripping each other's flesh. The flesh quickly healed as they stuck their tongues out to lick the ooze. Between the generations was a foul red pond of bellowing smoke, stretching from Great Bay to Grand Case.

Joaba clicked open his eyes. The maddening heat of the vision greased his face to a mirror's shine. He turned and walked toward the gate with a mission's stride.

"Before we know wha' happening, all the chil'ren we born come around to see wha' we doing here by weself. Vie didn't call them. Vie call Ademus's name."

"And he sen' dem to hear his story," yawned Doodey. "And this is what we all sitting up here way past moi bed toime to hear."

Mr. Priest, the sage from Marigot Hill, and Irad the mason, chuckled. Mr. Choisy, the statesman, patted Doodey's back.

"We ain goin' nowhere, Mr. Cyus," the Bush Lawyer contested broadly.

"Ademus story is the story of sacrifice for all that you lowe. When lowe leave you, when lowe scorn you, when you call lowe and lowe doan pay you no mind—it's your cross. Bear it like a man. If you a woman, bear it so. 'Causin when it sweet we lose time like chil'ren playing last-lick. Running ahead without the other to play hide-and-seek. We hurt and doan beg pardon. We doan forgive who wrong us. We covet and pretend to forget. Well, wha' miss you goin' catch yo' chil'ren.

"We doan take time to grow in lowe. We grow with yesterday pain and punish strangers for what they couldn't know happen to us. Sometime we self doan know what happen to us. We hoide behind rock walls of fantasy. Family secrets. Guilt. Shame. We run to church. We kick the life out of truth . . . lick loose trust before we take vows. In this turmoil, without knowing weself, we got the gall to go an' born an' rear chil'ren."

"Damn it, Cyus, it late. Done this blasted story once and fo' all," hawked out Viol.

The storyteller was unmoved. Lightning glared. "Ademus walked into what he couldn't know. Still, he was blessed. Look 'round you. All he chil'ren, gran' chil'ren, and too much family to mention, some from shores way away, are here tonight."

Widow Edonia knew from the dips in tone of Cyus's voice, from the leaps in pitch, which he called "mongoose and snake at it," that Ademus's favorite nephew was tired.

The hunger of these members of his tribe to hear Ademus's tale, as if it belonged to each one of them, had taken a toll on him.

Ademus marched sixty-three years, after his honorable discharge, into the century. It took the flogging and weals of a sapping sickness which came on without warning, to gather the tragic patriarch's kit and kin. Hours before his passing, delegations were still coming with missionary zeal from the external frontiers.

At death's portal, with Cyus's son the doctor attending like the ferry-man on the river Styx, Cyus at the foot of the bed garbed in priestly silence, and the dying man's congregation surrounding in a church of grief, Ademus closed his eyes and said absolutely nothing.

Now at his wake, it was with a seance of words that the living sought to invoke the meaning of his life, as if it would give their life greater meaning, new reason, to endure, to love, to build.

Cyus's heart pumped powerfully. He told the generations gathered that they were one family, one people, that they had been humiliated, and that agents of their humiliation still moved among them, dictating their direction, and that as a nation sacrificing was not enough. They also need love, courage, passion to claim their humanity, true identity, and their land.

"Hear the old mongoose and snake go at it," smiled the widow dimly to herself. She had long been veiled under her mosquito net. Daughters and granddaughters, Terez, and Mama Luce, the Haitian woman from whom she bought provisions at Marigot Market, kept checking on her. She laid on her back, eyes sealed, but not asleep. Though fatigued from the workings of the day, and before that from the dawn hours of Ademus's death, she tried to peal her ears to the story unveiling outside her bedroom window.

"Edonia . . ." The lightning seemed to reveal shadows about her room. The shudder of thunder appeared to echo voices. She thought it was Cyus who had called her name and was coming to say *bon nuit*. She opened her eyes wider. She could barely make out a shadow striding through

the children's room that separated her bedroom from that of her late husband.

Outside her room she could hear people saying good night to each other. Folks were telling her children to tell her good night, and to "take good care of her, becausin she all ahl yo' got now." Cyus was laughing and teasing Fondie about the mitigating effects of too much night dew on a man's prowess.

"Yes, Mr. Viol, ah goin' pick you up tomorrow to drive you to the burrying ground." That had to be one of Fondie's great-grands. They all had that heavy, judgment voice.

"I dozed off just like that? What could Cyus tell them? My God, why he mention Saysa for. He wasn't even born. What could Cyus tell about what I never talked to a mortal soul?" Edonia wondered to herself.

Cars were driving off, their headlights beaming with soft, steady breezes through the lining in the window, peeping in at the widow.

"Damn it, giol!" grizzled Viol on the porch, "Ahl yo' better walk meh home with this sin ah liquor soaked to meh soul." As he toiled out of his seat, he staggered into the reading chair, closer to the widow's bedroom window. The chair stiffened to the floor under his burden.

"What he just say?" wondered the woman under her net. "Good Father, I can smell the liquor on him."

"Edonia . . ." the familiar voice insisted. Lightning flashed pale. She sensed the approaching shadow and still thought that it was Cyus coming to say good night. "I got a good cuff for him for stirring up poor old Ademus to get all dem people listening to his preaching and politics," she thought to herself. "I doan know why he was not a politician and done."

"Come, nah," she called out. "And what does he know about sacrifice," she thought for a while. "He never had a hard day in his life. His father, mother, Samuel, and even Ademus took care of him. All of them gone except him. A wife and two children take good care of him now."

The shadow reached the foot of her bed.

A coldness overtook widow Edonia, froze her in a shiver. It was as though the fits of rage and fearful shadows lurking deep inside her, which haunted her every day and night, had just blown their icy breath to stifle her to death. Before her eyes she saw Saysa, her light, her honey-bunch flower, running past where she was hiding behind the rock wall. She saw herself as a five-year-old child. She was only pretending to run ahead, hands outstretched, lips pursed, buzzing like a bee.

Her sister's bare feet were thumping past her like a young mare, running into the sea. "For goodness sake," her eyes widened, "where is the rice bag full ah mangoes? Vie goin' eat we belly full on Friar's Bay Beach, right, Saysa?" The widow heard herself speak in a child's voice. Saysa was stepping back in the water, a giant white foam was grabbing after her.

"Damn it, giol, come here!" The drunken voice outside wrangled Edonia's gazing memory from the beach. A grin of lightning scurried through her net and refocused her memory on the crouching child that was she. The girl locked her tiny fingers around the widow's wrist and gently pulled the old woman behind a rock wall. The rocks were cemented with slimy, bulging-eyed-woodslaves.

"¡Esperate, señor!" snatched back a woman's voice outside, jerking the widow from the specter. It was the aged housekeeper of Viol and his crippled wife, asking the drunk to behave. Terez was helping her lift Viol, whose feet seemed shackled in a coma to Ademus's favorite chair. Viol was puked to his feet.

"Lucky thing we neighbors," grimaced Terez as the three struggled off the steps and down on the pavement under the weight of the drunken, cursing man.

The child's hand reappeared, this time fleshing through the mosquito net, welding into the widow's skin. A giant boat was waving out in the sea. Saysa fell under the water.

"Buh Saysa doan swim. How she hoidin under the water so loooong?" The widow's mouth formed the words being echoed by the little girl, both of them hiding behind the reptilian-lined rock wall. The foam turned around to face her. In its hand Saysa's panty. Its face was conked smooth like the back of a wet mouse. The giant boat was waving for the foam to come quick. The foam had a . . .

"Damn it, giol, come here! Oi'n finish with you yet!" came a grizzling voice from the sea, bursting the wall, shattering the hiding place. The eyes of the woodslaves splintered. Each eyeball sliver flashed the same picture of the hidden sin. A mighty current of blood flooded through the old woman.

She pulled the child into her. The shadows that hid deep inside and tortured her all these years had spoken!

Edonia screamed: "IT IS A MAAAAAAN!"

The widow's eyes goggled, and she convulsed in a gurgle of tongues. Her life arched over her. Each hole in the net became a mirror, reflecting a story. Gales of air were sucked into her, then palpitated out to cloud the mirrors which started splintering with a multitude of truths. A downpour of terrible coursing memories slammed and sank her into the bed. The mosquito net shattered with the renting jabs of her feet. The shadow calling her name was mounting the bed. Her breast bone was splitting from the pounding fury of blood thundering apart her heart's chambers, choking off the veins of air to her existence.

Cyus was visible now, his priestly eyes glowing amid the lamentation of voices and crying and praying and singing spreading through the door behind him.

She felt that she was telling him the truth. He would know how to tell this story. It did not have to be a family secret of ignorance anymore. She had found her sister's graveyard at last. She heard herself talking, saw everything and everyone in the room at once.

"Cyus, woi you ain answering me!? Viol rape an' drown meh sister. Why I hide it from meh-self? Woi Oi'n tell meh Daddie?!"

Edonia laid eyes on Hennee and felt such dreadful remorse that she moaned out her daughter's name. Pearl, now standing before her mother, turned and hammered her tear-sodden face in her own mother's breasts.

All that Edonia knew and dared not know and all the people there became as one . . . all things mattered to be set right . . . to be true . . . and time was the twitch of an eye. The shadow's hand formed out to her, it held her well, moved her along with a warrior's swiftness. It became her, drew her essence unto a saddle of light. She embraced it.

The prodigal stood at the gate when the widow's revelation came like a tidal wave to unclog arteries to a dead sea. Down the way he watched the shadow of Viol fall to its knees on the deeply gutted rocky road. The night wind whistled a curl of dust around the watcher's feet and set off with ghostly haste behind two silhouettes pulling another to its staggering feet.

"Damn it, leave me alone, you little bitch. I will kill you dead again!" came the maddening yelp from the knee-buckling Viol. He wrenched away from the two women and tried to run. Drunken, he rushed blindly into the barbed wire fence lining the path. The thorned wire shoved him back. Some part of him was heard to crack as he was dunked into the canyon of rockstones razoring up from the earth.

Joaba, prodigal son, watcher, turned away as the shrill screams of Terez and the housekeeper gushed past him like terrified phantoms.

He surveyed the sloping hills to the east, closed his eyes. He saw, in a tear of his vision, the dead which are not dead but yet memory, a brilliance of one that was yet all, gallop off the rim of sight.

"Edonia . . ." the vision called out.

Joaba heard a songful laughter like the breath of what must have been ten thousand bristling black stallions.

"Yes, Ademus . . ." came her wondrous voice of bliss.

Brotherhood of the spurs

He was lean. His crown was a fevered maroon red. His eyes, they say, pierced those of men to their gut and made women curse him as they would a demon son. His mouth was sharp and cutting, but he uttered no sound. His ears, his people swore, were cocked to the very rhythm of the great silence. His mane was a smooth gloss of black that shone as if coated with the fleece of crushed diamonds. His flesh was colored an iron rust that, they say, sprang from his very bones. His legs were waxed tight with an armor of yellowed gold. He wore razor-fine spurs of shell and stood like a warrior. He was home-hatched. They called him Browning.

The men of the maroon gathered for the third time that week under the tamarind tree overlooking Grand Case Beach.

"Vie say it got to be Browning," said Vaval as if setting a bird trap. He winked at old Duzant who sat, his back to the trunk of the bicentennial tamarind tree, right elbow propped on a walking stick Popo peeled from a coal kiln not one week ago.

Duzant could smell the smoke mixed with the fresh green from the tree-of-life that gave up its sturdy limb so that he might walk with grace alongside age. He inhaled and slapped his open left palm on his khaki-covered thigh. The sound rose like an applaud and stilled the waging tongues of the men who had all started arguing.

"Vie have to approach this like reasonable men, Vaval. Ven you rush us vie goin' make this decision like little boys playing in front they mother oize." He coughed and drew in breath to expel the itching and secret pain of his lungs. His red-veined eyes stung slightly, and at the coaxing by a hurried breeze sent from the sea, he blinked them dry.

"All ah us, one toime or another vie fight each other in the pit. T'ain 'gainst the law here, but ahl yu know ven vie fight in the bush pits, whether in Dutch Quarter or Guana Bay, t'gainst the law. Ahl yu men got good hands buh only one could make the champion vie need now."

"And only a fair fight goin' pick that real champion for the occasion we here for," spouted Sylvain.

The others nodded with an urgent flash of frowns and creasing brows.

Duzant raised his left hand like an elder chief. The veins of his raised hand caught a soft landing of sunlight. Mostly aged men were in the assembly. Vaval headed up the young set, and he was in his late thirties.

"Our way is to pick the best from among everybody to defend us. That is how it should always be among free men," returned Duzant with composure taught by the sea. He had hauled and mined by net and fish-pot his family's daily bread for fifty years.

"Flanders, Larmonie, Arnell, Richardson, Chance, Beauperthuy, Gumbs, Maccow, all the rest ah ahl yo', all ah we is here. Vie meeting like free men in the onliest village that does celebrate Schoelcher Day. Vie sitting down like one family becausin vie is one family. S'maatin is vie mother, and like Derio use to tell ahl yo, God and the Black man labor is this nation's true father." The gathering chuckled.

"Buh, Duce," called out Flem, with the

threat of humor at the base of his throat, "Wen yo' red like me and yo' grandfather is a Dutchman, wha yo' call me den?"

Flem's face flushed red over his freckles. The others scat and scattered in a temper of boyish laughter. Duzant raised his hand again. Sun-cast shadows dressed the old hand like a just polished mahogany bed post.

"Flem, vie all know your grandmother's name, and her father, bless him, wuz blacker than me. In S'maatin yu' know yo' one ah we. If yu go out in another world and they call yo' another name, and yu lose yo' way, man, just remember, in S'maatin yo' one ah we."

The words of the old fisherman composed the men as orderly as a school of silver fish appears before a net is cast on tranquil sea. A northeastern breeze fanned through the leaves of the ancient tamarind. The earth was drawing itself past the face of the sun.

"Meh boy, it goin' be hot tomorrow," forecast Beauperthuy as he raised his hawkish eyes to the west. Jagged dabs of orange set ablaze the sky. A drifting canyon of clouds sprayed a watercolor scarlet hovered over the horizon. Under this Master's canvas was resting the flat islandscape of Anguilla.

"And it is getting late," offered Barondi, fretting with the gold watch earned at the Lago refinery when he retired.

"If we ain able," continued old Duzant as if never interrupted, "to pick a *champene* by agreement today then tomorrow vie got to fight it out one for one. Then we goin' know once and for all who got the best cock in the land."

The pride of men bristled, hearts heaved, mouths dried, nostrils flared. They inhaled in the unison of a convent that sees its crimson tide in one flow. They exhaled as if not to disturb each other's thoughts.

"Damn it then. It about time," flung Flem with an irreverence that disturbed the older heads, but found a wildcat consent among the younger generation.

"Let's go one for one," he charged, bristling with the bull-headed disrespect of old man Bell's cattle when crossing Union Road in front of traffic. He had the upper hand. He would sweep in the motion the younger men smelled blood for.

"Let's do it that way," they chanted.

"Browning goin' beat 'em all anyway," said Vaval, unable to keep the fire of youth from burning down the bridge across the years of lessons learned in the matter at hand.

"Done those days of exhibition, showing off some old gore who ain win a fight in years."

"Yeah, foolin' people about he too good to fight in S'maatin anymore. That we got to save him for outside challenges."

"Chups."

"Becausin vie goin' see now whose cock is man and who got hen and callin' him cock."

The voices of impatience and youth, left out of the learning and culturing of aged secrets, ruled.

The gathering disbanded with unfamiliar commotion.

Over the next weeks, families of the great fighting cocks guarded their wire coops, groomed their proud he-fowls in the manner accustomed to each, fed them the purges that puked out the slime of sickness and clots of bruised blood, massaged them with particular care, offered them meals of sustenance and water clean and pure, whispered missives of battles and glory, administered psychic martial codes. Some had spurs mounted by masters of ancient crafts and others summoned with equal secrecy the sprinkle of holy water and other blessings by priests, practitioners, and ministers of a region of faiths. There were those who imported spurs of steel and sapatong while others fashioned theirs from shell and according to the traditions of their fathers.

All had formulas and amulets and tales and ways of handling what amounted to chants for victory.

Throughout the weeks of preparation, a series of cockfights took place to determine the defending champion. One by one each family alighted in the small and great pits the finest of their feathered legion to challenge and be challenged.

"Leh meh tell ahl yo', up to now, it nothing but feathers and blood and grown men, big and small, crying deyself to sleep at night. They come like babes in dey mother arms," lashed out Loulouze in Marigot Market. It was Saturday. The last championship test would take place the following day.

"This thing has gone too far, my dear girl, but it is the sport of the time and the people love it," pitched in Ma'm Barondi from her usually up-nosed countenance.

"Mmmm," injected Titeen with mock surveillance of her large wooden tray of ground provision and fruit. Of all the market women, her garden's harvest was most coveted from Grand Case to Great Bay.

The market woman's utterance dug an ominous trench around the women. The quietness anchored Ma'm Barondi's unusual desire to chit-chat in an impoverished gut of silence. Out of the blue, Gussyann's daughter stumbled through the conference's stalemate. The girl tumbled Titeen's pyramid of yams into parcels of sugar apples, pushing the ripe-sweet apples onto the long, coarse cassava roots.

"Child, be careful," fretted the market woman. Without missing a beat, she began reshaping her produce. "There's an order to things."

"Miss Titeen, sorry fo' knocking down yo' things, buh meh mudder sen meh to ask you fo' the bush tea you promise her. Meh faader still cahn sleep and he getting up shouting that he cock dead and he cahn fight in the war of judgment."

"Dis ting gone too faah, meh dear giol!" carried on Loulouze, hands akimbo.

Titeen looked up at her and sucked her teeth severely, cut up her eyes, and turned her head away.

"Mmmm," incited Ma'm Barondi.

The frenzied talk of cockfighting resumed.

Titeen, like the eye of a hurricane, drew a worn folding of sheep's skin from her bosom, unfolded it with her farmer's hands, parceled four leaves with a gentle weaning, parted her lips, raised to her full carving of lips the black and silver crucifix that rested on her ample right breast, kissed it, and let it fall. The crucifix slapped the perspiration glean of cocoa-rouge skin. Loulouze heard the sting of cross upon flesh.

Gussyann's daughter drew to the market woman's side and knelt beside her. She could not remember if Titeen had called her or motioned for her to come.

"Tell yo' mother doan boil de water too long this toime and give it to him befo' he go sleep. Buh he cahn eat after that. You hear?"

"Yes, Miss Titeen," answered the awkward almond-eyed child.

"Da's a noice mammy giol," soothed Titeen after kissing the young forehead. She pressed the green leaves, wrapped in a torn piece of wax paper, in the left palm of Gussyann's daughter. The doctorwoman gently clasped the adolescent fingers over the cure.

Loulouze broke the bonding.

"Wha yu giving that choil there?"

"Yu come here to boi green bananas fo' yo'

family or live up to other people's words," flung back Titeen fiercely.

"Wha yu' mean now?!"

"Meh choil, chicken and guinea bird only walk together when guinea bird wing is broken."

"Whoooooo! Ah yo' Lord!" moaned Loulouze with feigned innocence. She glanced at Ma'm Barondi, encircled by a whirl of tongues from towns and villages. When Loulouze faced Titeen, the childhood friends collided in an eye-watering fit of laughter.

"So Titeen, meh dear, who goin' be vie champene?" She stood, hands akimbo, as if daring an answer other than what should be.

"Lord, Loulouze, woi yu gotta ask meh dat?"

"It Oi, Loulouze, asking yu!"

"Browning." The answer was resolute.

Loulouze sucked her teeth in protest and started feeling up the green bananas.

Titeen, unaffected, weighed a parcel of tania and yam handed her by Mrs. Cannegieter.

"Browning my foot!" lunged Mrs. Cannegieter uninvited. "He is a black demon. God will smite him for all the sins of gambling."

The market woman offered the church woman her parcel and thanked her most kindly for her pay. Thereafter came Ma'm Barondi, wiping with unaccustomed abandon a wet, red flowered handkerchief across the continent of her brow. She pushed her grin-flushed face over Titeen's tray and ordered her provision with a sweeping gesture of her other hand.

As the woman left the market with much lightness of foot and swaying of hips upon a leggo of high-heeled feet, the sun mounted noon with a beastly coupling of heat and light over the weekly bayside intercourse.

Gussyann's husband, Mossy, lost all of his fine feathered breed the week before his wife ordered the second prescription from Titeen. He lost his money by training, gambling, and ordering a hear-about fighting breed from abroad. He lost the money his sister had been sending from Aruba for him to finish her house in Sucker Garden before Christmas. The retired policeman took to his bed. He had refused to take Titeen's tea with pig-like grunts, while calling names Gussyann remembered as the number sellers he had arrested with such abusive glee in Curaçao.

After inhaling the aroma of tea prepared this time by his daughter, Mossy drank it all and drowsed away. Around midnight, visions battled him with terror-inspiring force from sleep to preachment. His babbling drove Gussyann into the yard and away from the light of the kerosene lamp. She stumbled into the full moon-soaked yard hours after the nightly switch-off of electricity in Great Bay.

The daughter, who had imitated Titeen's lips and hand gestures while preparing the prescription, stayed, sat on a stool at the foot of her parents' bed, head bowed, palms clasped, lips moving swiftly, silently.

Mossy sermonized from atop his mount of pillow. His toes spiked down as if he was being dangled from the ceiling by a horrid puppeteer's strings, his hands stretched out like a cross.

"Mammy, he say that Browning goin' win for we," professed the child the morning after.

"Jesus Christ. The man finally crazy," whispered the wife, eyes glazing into the direction of the bedroom. Her night was spent between checking on Mossy after he cooled down and her sleeping rose of a daughter, and hurrying back to her sister next door. Her sister kept the vigil with stories of madness, convincing Gussyann that her husband was a lunatic.

"Daddy say to prepare fo' victory and that the day of judgment is at hand and that Browning will rise from the pit to put his enemies to shame, win back we money, and unite the brotherhood of the spurs." The girl told this with the stolidness of a seer doomed never to be believed.

"Brotherhood of what? Cassandra, it look like your father mek you gone crazy too!" exclaimed the mother, pushing past the daughter and storming the bedroom. On the bed lay her husband prostrated in a fatigue of sleep.

That Sunday afternoon, as Mossy stirred awake, the cockfighters gathered far away for the day of the judgment. Sylvain named it so. The day of the battle, out of which two birds would be left. The defending champion would be the cock that won the last round.

In the fullness of the afternoon, Mossy felt fine. By the time he rose from his bed, took a cold shower, ate a little something, dressed dapperly, kissed his daughter, teased his wife about her grey hair, and set off for the cockfight, the judgment was in full swing. Round and round went the fighting he-fowls. Round and round went the men and cadre of women in a continuous casting of bets and lots, heaving themselves in a fast of silence and raging fits.

Family and friends spoke through the fierce, proud piercing eyes of their cocks. Each rooster, neck arrogantly stretched, stoically pointing his beak around, rallied a nation under the banner of his tail, lording over his troop's lust for glory until he was himself routed, taken limp, fluttering, or dead from the pit.

Some elders who came brisk and bold to the cockfight had to be led from the pit's edge to the bush by cane or comrade to relieve the movement of their bowels.

Men, fierce of face, mirrors of ancient warriors, and some with that old maroon spirit, some who had a bull force voice and hands iron-strong from honest and hard labor, all were by now drained and unknown to each other. Bullies were bowed. Women who could box off any man wept sorely over the loss of their cocks, eyes reddened, bodies slouched, and sweated like the particular rooster that had driven them to this downcast of spirit.

When the judgment round came upon the mass, a matte of blood and mucus and feathers had to be swept from the pit by two brooms of twigs and leaves. A wind blew a dust-laden mist of hot blood and fowl flesh to the nostrils of the people. Able sons swept and swept sods of feathers and life's fluids over the grave pit's rim.

Only two clans were erect now. They strutted, their voices bellowed, their eyes stared, their hands raised and fisted the air, their nerves and muscles pumped a fever-mad charge of iron blood. The air became inflamed with a contagion that soon raised the dead and dying armies of the vanquished to choose new sides.

The wind breathed new life in the assembled and each side chanted that the last bout of judgment would now be theirs alone and only theirs.

As the generals inspected their cocks, stroked their heads, beaks and chests, and sprayed a tonic mist from their mouths into their birds' faces, onto their breasts, under their wings, the betting sparred with deadly order and aim. In the dizzying din of swears and warnings, jests and last minute desertions, the *impis* cocked their heads with unaffected disdain. The warrior cocks were the eyes among these hurricane people and became their spirit and body.

Duzant held his hand barely above his head. Silence squeezed humanity from the air. A cast of shadow from a head of clouds buffed the glare of sun. Duzant leveled his hand downward. The last two feathered fighters were presented to the pit's war-blistered field.

One army stomped and thumped the ground with earthquake feet, batted finger and money and cane and handkerchief and whatever was held in its alarmed hands, warningly, pleadingly, at its terrible eye of the storm. The martial band ranted, raved, and roared, "BATTLE RED!"

The other army slapped its aroused chests, jabbed the air with fists, canes, currencies, and broomsticks. The multitude towered and thundered, "BROWNING!"

Before touching the ground, both roosters began glaring and spiking and spearing. Tunfoot Giggi, on his knees, hands clasped in prayer, a phantom dust buzzing around him, was the first to witness. He held his head in a vice of fright.

"It de win', de win', de win' takin' heem up in de air!"

Hyman, who organized this fight under the almond tree, rushed the pit with his fist of francs and guilders and dollars renting space for him to pass, bawling out: "That is a demon! That is a demon!"

As Duzant rose from the rickety bench, younger men flung themselves to the ground, rolling in the dust, some with choked laughter, some in a comess of curses.

Mossy appeared at the bush pit's entrance.

Browning began to descend, his wings waxed sharp like a silver cross, his eyes pitiless. His left spur, spitting a blinding sparkling of sunlight, stretched down stealthily from his lean body, his right leg prepared as claw or landing gear.

Battle Red, not yet touching ground, looked up.

Browning's general guided at a psychic pitch: "Fall faster, steep right spur, swipe air upward, slice skin of neck, cut feather apron under throat, avoid beak, jag eye, twist, pull, drop weight, crush head, avoid enemy's dying kicks. Done him."

"What you say happen?" reared Gussyann through her kitchen door hours after the judgment.

"I said," repeated her sister, spacing her words further apart for clarity. "Emma-say-people-run-from-de-pit-holding-dey-head-and-dey-belly-and-bawling-murder!

"Then Duzant tell Gibbs to call Guadeloupe and tell them S'maatin ready!"

Gussyann sucked her teeth and slammed her door shut. "All ah dis damn foolishness because some drunken Guadeloupean made a bet last Christmas that St. Martin could never find a champion to beat de Guadeloupe champion."

Her muttering picked up steam as she moved

from kitchen to dining room to living room to bedroom to bathroom. "I bet Mossy still with that bunch of cockfighting no-goods. Some got the heart to call themselves gentlemen and fighting cocks on the Lord's day. I never hear more. Last night, Mossy ranting and raving, nearly scared me to death.

"He got he nerves to go cockfight after he lost he will and worth to the damn foolishness. Wait 'till Guadeloupe come cut dey tail good."

Gussyann had decided to bet her little savings and return to Curaçao, with or without Mossy. She had sworn never to return to the St. Martin where her mother had passed such shame for not knowing for sure who was Gussyann's father. The damn Sing Sing island, she condemned, barely had electricity and, she swore again, would stay backward forever.

Gussyann scurried back to the kitchen, opened the top half of the split-level door and peered over at her sister's house. She could hear the laughter and clapping and shouting and teasing. She squinted, counting Emma, who raised he-fowls and hosted bullfight dances, Gracie from Anguilla, Esther-Ruth from Saba, Goldie from Statia, all seated around the kitchen table in a sweet-looking fête of familiarity.

"*Dushi.*"

"Yeah, Mammy," answered her daughter who was picking limes from the tree in the backyard.

"Go tell *tante* she ain even say who win."

"Buh, Mammy, Daddie say . . ."

"Look, choil, do what I say."

"Well, what dey say?" inquired Duzant.

"Duce, well, I came to tell you first like you ask me a week ago," answered Gibbs. "I know it a bit late in the night, but I only just get the answer from *Monsieur* Felicien Tourbain in Guadeloupe."

"Okay," waited Duzant, bringing his rocking chair to attention on its toes. "When?"

"They say they will be here in two weeks."

The next morning after church, the cockfighters gathered under the shade of the tamarind tree planted by their ancestors.

"Ah tell ah yo' it got to be Browning. Buh Oi ain here to brag and boast. Vie all fight like men. One ah meh best fighting cocks dead when Barondi set he white spaniel on him. Buh a week after he found he oan *gallo hiero* in that mahga fowl Mossy bring in from St. Thomas."

Everyone laughed that kind of laughter like

veterans remembering fallen comrades. One champion gambler called Rogers slapped Mossy on the back reassuringly.

"Now the bet I made with a man who had too much guavaberry in moi oan house last year and bring us all to this has got to be paid up," issued Barondi soberly.

"Barondi, this is not the first time you had the good sense of a jackass," intervened Duzant. An orchestra of nodding heads and a pan-yard of grumbling ensued.

"You got land and business like yo' family always had all over this oilan buh yo' mouth and ambition is a trouble and burden. A lot ah men lost more than yu'll ever give back. Buh vie went in this for sport, the challenge, and becausin vie honor vie cocks and love S'maatin, and not a damn soul should challenge a S'maatin man in he house and get away with it."

"I know Felicien," protested Vaval. "He a honest man. Real level-headed. He been buying good cattle in S'maatin since I small, from the Balys, the Bells. All ah ahl yo' know that. I ain so sure he was that drunk."

Barondi turned his head toward the sea, coughed and spat nervously.

"Maybe Barondi only telling us his side of

the story, and we all pay already, nearly kill all we best breed. Now we could be shamed for a long time by dem Guadeloupeans.

"Dey'll never let us live it down and for what! Heh? Tell me, for who?"

"Let bygones be bygones, Va. Is the fight Oi wahn now," offered Beauperthuy. "Everybody united. Vie one S'maatin family. Browning is vie champene."

There was a rousing round of voices and gestures, arguments and agreements.

Duzant's niece came with a long crystal tray filled with assorted glasses containing lime and rum punches, cognac, and all the select spirits of the brotherhood.

They went on deep into the afternoon, soothing pride, smoothing feathers, setting place, date, time.

News of the cockfight spread off the island like wildfire by letters, telephone, and telegrams. Sailors, fishermen, and traders carried the news to neighboring islands. Breeders from throughout the cockfighting Caribbean called up their old friends and kinsmen to be invited and to invite themselves. Men of business and government invited their colleagues from the region.

Not since the great stickfight between

Quashi the Rambaud defender and the Kittitian champion had the villages and towns of St. Martin been so rallied in a fête of oneness in which the sacrifice of pride and name was set upon an altar of chance and game.

The blood-fever of the brotherhood, the contagion of the pit raged across the sea. Betters from Trinidad, Puerto Rico, the Cubans from Miami, and St. Martiners from Aruba and New York began coming in, upping the stakes beyond what those of Anguilla, Saba, Statia, St. Kitts, St. Lucia, Antigua, and St. Barths had pilgrimaged to contest. Some begged and borrowed. Some called home or sent messages any which way they could to have more money sent. Many more visitors arrived carrying cash and more excitement to feed the blood game.

The brotherhood moved the fight from the selected Saturday to Sunday because the challenger's special steel spurs from France were going to be a day or two late, relayed Gibbs. Time would be needed to adjust *"les éperons."*

When Mrs. Cannegieter's reverend would not condemn the sport on the sabbath, she threatened to pull her family out of the church and drag off some church sisters and most of the choir with her. She was one of the very few who opposed the fight with Bible-thumping, rosary-slinging fervor. The shepherd of the flock spoke to her great uncle. The old battle spur, whose prized Cuban black smuggled to him by Hazel had been a fatality, reminded his grandniece that his will included her mother. That calmed the church lady's righteous indignation.

The Saturday before the fight, the Guadeloupeans marched out of Juliana Airport's arrival hall, surrounding their he-fowl like stone-faced guardians would a potentate, pope, president, or prize-fighter.

St. Martiners cheered the challengers with such vim and vitality that guest betters and visitors on hand would later spread word of "the friendly island people."

Felicien and his St. Martin friends embraced as long lost brothers. He introduced the members of his delegation to the welcoming party. Some knew each other from previous cockfight tournaments held between the two islands.

The welcoming delegation was headed by Barondi, his enormous belly preceding him wherever he turned to greet the blood sport brothers. Only a few shook hands at this encounter. There could be strong magic about. Some of the visitors raised their other cocks out of the cages as decoys to prevent too many eyes being cast on their champion. Every one nodded with respectful exuberance. Most of the Guadeloupeans wore a serious countenance. St. Martiners, on the other hand, were smeared with that smile they wear sometimes, as if they have a paradise secret to share with everyone, but no one is paying attention.

The visiting delegation was spirited away in a motorcade of three cars driven by compatriots who lived in St. Martin.

The following day, at the grounds of the last great maroon ever held in French Quarter, the warriors were weighed in at eight o'clock in the morning. A knight's table of breakfast was prepared for the people who gathered early: saltfish with thin, soft cucumber slices and diced onion, johnnycakes, hot bakes with butter dripping warm as they were bitten into, jelly for bread, mackerel, steaming bush teas stirred with brown sugar from St. Kitts, cocoa tea from Dominica, coffee that was picked from up in Hope Estate and grounded in Grand Case, creamy porridges made, not with water, but with the milk from Gaspard Baly and Flemming's fat-titty cattle. Cinnamon and nutmeg from Grenada were stuck in or grated over corn or arrowroot pap.

Folks, some with their children, trailed back and forth between the maroon encampment and Coconut Grove. They passed without saluting the salt ponds of their foreparents' unreparated labor.

As morning opened further, there were boat, donkey, and horse races. Lovers swam out far into the ocean and undressed each other under the water. Children ran and jumped and laughed, and men and women were like children again, bursting with jokes and rolling with laughter and playing jumping bag and egg-in-spoon competition and all that marvelous foolishness each generation comes to swear gave to its own the best time on earth.

Philip and Elick butchered thirty-seven animals from their finest stock of cattle, flock of sheep, herd of goats, and pen of pigs.

Following the midday battle, the banquet tables would be laid before the society. All were welcome and all would partake today. The colorful cloth-decked tables were laden with fowl, whelk, lobster, conch, goat fish, yellow-tail, jacks, red snapper, crab and rice, and stewed pigeon peas on the side, dumplings stewed in milk, and fresh callaloo and rice. Lokrio, too.

From Colombier they brought yam, tania,

cassava, and sweet potato. Salads galore from Middle Region to Cripple Gate were dressed with vinegar, salt, black pepper, sweet oil, and lime juice. And again, saltfish, fixed all kinds of how, and johnnycake. There were stewed chicken, souse, cow heel soup, peas soup, goat meat, stewed mutton, beef, and roasted corn.

People would cool their thirst with frosty soursop juice, mauby, tamarind, passion, sorrel, and lime juices; lime punch and liqueur, Beauperthuy Punch, Melford lemonade, and guavaberry. Dessert would follow with cakes and bakes and sweet buns. There were peppermint candy, coconut sugarcakes, and peanut drops, roasted peanuts and cashews.

Whoever did not bring a picnic basket could buy or be treated to a feast of food, for after the great battle would come the traditional repast. And after the feast would come the bullfight dance.

Now the sun mounted noon, and the main cockpit crowed open.

The assemblage from afar seated at will among the friendly people. The camps and their crowding armies were seen, known, and pointed out to all. The din of betting clamored before awestruck children, who were pointing out to each other who was who and what was what.

The preliminary bouts of bloodlust had only whetted the betters' appetites.

The church leaders all came, "to see that the children were not in harm's way."

Short khaki-pants gendarmes might have even forgotten they were from France for this bliss moment.

The Dutch and French governors of the two occupying states seated themselves next to each other with familiarity. Flanking them were assorted men of government, as well as their wives or traveling sweethearts from Saba, Statia, St. Barths, St. Kitts, Anguilla, Antigua, Guadeloupe, Martinique, St. Thomas.

School teachers and men and women of business sat aside men who handled fishnet and women who once picked salt and rocks to lay the airport runway. They addressed each other as Miss This and Mister That and inquired about an old aunt or grand uncle who was probably sitting about two rows in the back or front or at the pit's ringside.

The political boss, who was also a doctor, was there. He pretended not to notice the newspaperman he had banned from crossing the border. Some of the same people who not long ago swore at the political rally that they were going to shoot the crusading voice were encircling him with embraces, back slaps, offering news, views, food, drink, and flamboyant smiles.

The other political bossmen were in their usual drunken spree and tom-foolery, casting lots as they had become adept at doing so well.

"Well, Duce, the respectable families and all are here," mused Vaval.

"Well yes, *primo*, you know we are all respectable people," answered Duzant pridefully. From atop his seat he was judge and apparent holder of the peace that tied cycles of pit chaos to reverent order.

Titeen, Loulouze, Gussyann, and Mrs. Cannegieter were there too.

Then it came. Just so. As sudden as the summit of such events appear when all assembled know the appointed hour and each his assigned and assumed place.

Hounded from giving his own speech, "becausin t'ain no election toime," Barondi prevailed on the brethren to let Ma'm Barondi, his daughter, do the honors.

"Dignitaries, ladies and gentlemen, people of S'maatin. Friends from overseas. Our guests and challengers from Guadeloupe. *Bienvenue, Bienven-*

ido, Welkom, Welcome!

"This is the day we all have been talking about for so long. We have our champion, excuse me, our champene as the children say. His name is Browning! Our guests all say it must be a nansi story how Battle Red met his end. Battle Red is dead! Today all will see who will leave the pit as champion! Everybody is saying it will be a long and hard fight.

"Good luck to all. May all S'Maatiners and you, our dear friends, remember this bright and sunny day, with this fresh breeze blowing in from the sea, for a long time."

A vigorous hand-clapping and whistling marshaled back to urgency the business at hand.

The fighters were at the pit, held high by their generals, not as trophies but as centurions would a Caesar, select warriors would an *Asanthane*, or paraders would a Garvey.

Titeen looked over, a quarter of a circle away, at Duzant. He immediately tipped his old panama brim to her. She kissed her cross. When Loulouze heard it slap back to Titeen's breast she looked askance at her childhood friend. They cut up eyes, raised their right eyebrows as they did when nervous, smiled anxiously, held hands reassuringly, and gazed prayerfully upon Browning.

Ma'm Barondi glanced at the strange acknowledgment between Titeen and the old maroon judge. Some current from the sighting caused her skin to crawl and raise in a blanket heat of prickly bumps. The glance transfixed her, as if she had no business bearing witness to it. It locked her in a timeless moment, standing between her seated father to the right and to her left, Duzant, his lifelong partner of the pit.

Around this triad, sealed in place and time by a rite of the medicine woman's eyes, were circles deep of families forged by centuries, and friendships forged through life-long days, and blood, and political alliances. And those circles spread out to encircle more families and acquaintances and villages and visitors and made space across from the brotherhood nucleus to the challengers, kindred in the game and in the region of engagement.

The bandera tails of the spurred cocks were whispering in the afternoon breeze and salt scent.

Ma'm Barondi's skin crawled full of chicken-flesh again. She had felt this chilling heat a few weeks ago while leaving the market, so elevated in spirit and full sweetness of body. She thought the deadness felt within that drove her home—

from where she still called her *métropole*—to seek refuge from a pale lover's spurn would be an eternal thirst, never to be slaked.

Here, now, at the rim of the pit, her hips abandoned their studied composure and swayed loose to one side. Her long legs, ever so softly, opened like a morning glory. Her right hand left the shoulder of her father and flew to akimbo.

Duzant raised his scepter hand above his head. Silence squeezed from a humanity of over one thousand souls. Wide-eyed children pointed out to each other the chieftains of the game. In some homes these blood sport men were spoken of as if they were larger than life. Children looked upon them as giants who kept scores of fighting birds caged in sky castles, scaled only in the tales of rudies and tomboys.

Today, as ever, the game cocks never glanced at the generals who so reverently fashioned them for combat. Not once did the prized he-fowls bestow a look of grace upon the armies harnessed under the banderole of their tails.

Not so much as a nod to knight the throngs who adored their prowess, who invoked their name, who found the fleeting spirit to strike, to strength, to stride, through their fatal victories.

These sights to behold, thus, then, and there,

were eyes of these hurricane people who galed around them.

Duzant lowered his hand. He felt a needling pain shoot out from its secret place in his breast bone and solder his fingers in a sweaty union.

The two spurred gladiators were presented to the arena. One set of the challenger's army yielded its studied French to its nation's Patois of songful passion. The whole huddled, *la-lwa-di*. Then the formation danced loose, pounded separate fists into separate palms and yelled out what sounded like warnings. They chanted furiously, "VINI, FRANÇOIS SAN BLÉY!"

It was the first time that most of the maroon's inhabitants had heard the challenging champion's name.

The troops of the host army slapped their chests, pressed their breasts, stomped the ground with earthquake feet, batted and fisted the air, flung high fingers, white-gloved hands, hats, canes, and currencies. They shouted, roared, bristled, and thundered, "BROWNING!"

All pointed with cyclonic yells to the silent, seasoned warriors.

Before touching the ground, both cocks glared and spiked and picked. Both arched their bodies and lanced forward, crown to crown, puffed chest to puffed chest, and hung brazenly in the air, eye to eye, beak to beak—*épée à épée!*

The congregation rose to revival abandon, babbled up to God to bless their own, and demanded of the devil to be done with the other.

Mrs. Cannegieter lost her glove under the dust-stuffed benches.

Ma'm Barondi, in a ground sea of excitement, felt the snap of her brassiere as a drench of sweat flooded scales of age off her heart.

Vaval vaulted at the pit with hara-kiri madness. A stampeding crop of teenagers rode his back to the brink of the rink.

A phalanx of Kwéyòl lanced out from the challenging legion, leaped to the pit, pressing onto the visiting general's back, lashing him with a labyrinth of *lewoz* tongues.

Tunfoot Giggi was on his knees, palms appealing upward, a swirl of dust spiraling about him. Tears washed his cheeks into a matte of tribal marks. He saw it coming as clear as day, and he screeched a lunatic's howl. Gussyann's daughter, Cassandra, rushed to peer over the cripple's shoulders.

Titeen read the child's telling face.

"Wha' wrong, Titeen!" demanded Loulouze, "Oi cahn see good. All this dust and commotion.

Wha'wrongwithyu!Woiyusostiff?!"

The medicine woman stood in a fit-like *pris-des-yeux*, tranced between her friend's gripping and pulling and the drawing account of the savage art.

"OhLawdOhLawd! It de spike! De spike! He goin' spike heeeeeem!" heralded Tunfoot Giggi.

Flem appeared suddenly and raised a stiff-bodied Duzant to his feet. Beads of perspiration sprang through the old judge's balding crown, rained over his forehead and rivered down his back. His left hand clutched his chest as he would a marlin clutching for the air of the sea. Ma'm Barondi wiped his aged brow with her sweat-soaked, perfumed handkerchief.

Browning began to ascend, unbelievably, higher, his left leg taking aim. His wings waxed a bewitching silver in the span of a cross.

His general's whisper was psychic: "Cockspur. Razor through breast. Spike wing across head. Cut crown, blood-spill-hot-run, blinding him. You are invisible. Claw neck, loose and send in deathmount spur. He is falling. Jag eye. Twist. Pull. Let dead weight drop. Return."

François San Bléy splattered to the ground with a thud that earned a moment of reverent quiet for the noble fallen.

Barondi relieved a waterfall of sweat from his face.

Children held their breath in disbelief.

The Guadeloupean general's mouth opened bitterly: "*Djab!*"

Gussyann closed her eyes to a frigid Judas pain.

Browning alighted on his general's trunk-like arm with a fierce gripping. He had not yet touched the ground. The feminine Lenten breeze stroked him at the skin under his feathers. His claws mined maroon blood from the general's level veined arm of cosmic black. Life fluid streamed from flesh to pit's ground. Browning's wings raised, as Pegasus in flight, away from his burning, iron-blood-pumped body. The cropped feathers about his neck were stiffly still as the hair on the neck of a snarling yard dog. A white handkerchief was waved out of the mist of dust at the general. He received it with priestly calm and wiped the wet rubies of sacramental blood from the under part of his arm.

Now Browning eyed them. There, see how they carried on, the bacchanalian heaping, heaving carnivalesque of human host that had set him on high. He, apis bull. He, golden calf. He, soapstone bird. He, gargoyle. He, plumed serpent. He, Shango icon. He, hubris. He leveled his perch on the bâton arm. Alone. Proud. Merciless. Perfect.

Daniel Zebedee Duzant crossed to the other side that night. Dr. Victor said the old fisherman's heart gave out from too much excitement.

Browning disappeared before the crowing in of dawn which greeted the day of Duzant's funeral. The rope latch to his coop door was cut loose. Some say he was stolen. Some say Duzant's spirit took him beyond the grave.

"He wasn't of this world anyway," swore Loulouze in a whisper. She made a quick sign of the cross while crushing her eyebrows into tight folds.

A new procession of mourners greeted and parted Titeen and Loulouze and entered the hall to sit with the widow following her beloved's burial.

"And how would you know that?" resumed Titeen with the conspiratorial whispering.

The woman, who knew the secrets and healing season of herbs, sat with her old friend on the small verandah. She eyed the circle of men under the ancient tamarind tree, silhouetted into the shadows of twilight. The younger men had long gone about their business. Now the old fellows will raise the memory of Brother Duce and rest him their way.

Titeen rested back in Duzant's chair and rocked an evocative rhythm of gentle softness.

Loulouze looked knowingly upon her dear friend's ageless and perfectly calm face. Both began humming a hymn of goodly praise with even gentleness.

FIRESPILL

Akillah Lakshmih was elected president in an age of great threats and rumors of threats. Yet it was an age seething with the marvelous fruits of human reason and harvests of science in post-gigabyte drive.

Her country was the equatorial crossroads of transbloc trade and the last hold-out of old-fashioned offshore financial secrecy. She, like her predecessors, was rumored to be flirting a favoritism with the age's reigning terror—which was rumored, more than once, to have sent its mercenaries to protect the pride of the century's city-islands from some rapacious interest, or to frustrate to futility another outpost corrective transbloc legislation from being enforced by E-POLI, the Earth Police Interactive.

Criss-crossed as the country was by the world, no path had cut through it deeper than the ancient line that divided the people's integrity and defied reason. Lakshmih was her country's first president elected with a mandate to defy the division of no reason and seek a union once and for all.

It was well-rumored that it was she, herself, who cultured sponsorship of the mandate among her father's old commercial constituency. Now its members spoke of "the prosperous and sacred union" as their personal own. Captains of the constituency found consensus with a largely beleaguered and dispossessed brethren across the frontier.

The chief executive did not know how she would engage and execute the union process, given the odds. What she was certain of was that the crafting of pretext and possibilities was well within her domain.

Had not her great-grandfather crafted the pretext of partition from the Antilles colony and forged independence for the republic?

Had not his successor cultured the infamous possibilities with the trade cartels of his time that kept great powers from overrunning the new nation?

Had he not groomed the securing of elbow room for her determined people?

Had not that cleared ground enabled her nation to plant the bold and brave seeds of prosperity, making so much possible so fast?

And had her father for naught carved a cutting-edge niche for the convergence of transbloc trade in and out of NAFTASPHERE and, rumored as it still is, quickly convinced "The Terror" of its interest in protecting pre-century offshore banking in St. Martin?

This first year of her four-year term attracted more commercial transshipment than any other time in the city-island's history. For the first time, those claiming multinational citizenship to escape transbloc taxation, outstretched the immigrant influx. Trimester-stay tourists were increasing quarterly like never before.

The abundance of material prosperity made up the bed for great leisure but was marginalizing incentives to pursue the immaterial values of civilization, and thus the immortality of the individual's deeds and name.

The president's vidphone chimed. A nine-inch liquidy hologram of a news reporter laser-beamed up from table-center. Both communication links interrupted the Executive Cabinet of

Ministers' meeting. This was the early week's third tête-à-tête on how to keep the Brazilian and South African bankers from clashing again with Benelux Republic co-financiers and that aggressive globe-trotting lot of Cubaïti engineers. The prize? The mega-billion creditdollar sub-extension of the Transhemispheric Great Bay Port.

THE PORT WILL BE TOUCHING SABA BY 2100, ended the fourth morning headline from http://www.earth-news.sm.com. The reporter beamed back into the egg-shaped module at table-center.

"That's all the American sub-marine gas miners need to hear. Soon they will start whining again about offshore jurisdiction," clipped Vice President Massif York.

"Off E-News St. Martin," he commanded, preempting the quarterly hour headline interruptions.

The president linked her vid to conference audio-visual.

"President Lakshmih," rushed out the caller's face and voice from the table-center module, "it's Dr. Sixto Arrindell again! He's getting real *opstandig*. He called, faxed, e-mailed, AND three-D'd his big forehead face. I blocked his sub-sentext to you. Now he is threatening a viral hour feed! You know what happened last week when Translinxx Union viral hour feed was sent through security bank central and crashed its modem for three days? Huh.

"And E-POLI micro-sentext another warning this morning since nobody in this government has chosen to answer their last two micro missives. They say that if we can't handle a little union, they will . . ."

"Okay, Okay, Jennifari. Enough! I will see Dr. Arrindell at noon," consented the president tiredly.

"Why do we put up with these viral feeds, receptionists who bypass executive commissioners to interrupt ECM meetings, and just about anybody feeling they can storm through the halls of national government, demanding to see President, minister of cabinet, legislative councilor, senator?" flared Minister J. P. Méran.

"Another thing. Every other country in the working world has outlawed viral feeds and given E-POLI jurisdiction over offenders. Why haven't we?"

"Méran, openness is what has always made St. Martin work. Viral feeds are certainly part of our people's democracy. They let people put in check the light-year speed of what little is left of public accountability. Besides, they are harmless computer byte interruptions."

"Harmless, no, Madame President," rushed in Vice President York. "Last year a vhf held up your inauguration on Globe-Spann, CNN, and E-News for five broadcast attempts. It cost us five million creditdollars in fines. All because the resort maids, MAIDS, wanted to REMIND you that you PROMISED to meet with them first after taking office."

"But, York," sparred Minister of Education and Culture Nadikwa James, "who was that young sensational candidate about fifteen years ago who viral-fed his demands to the Electoral Congress? I believe he called for a switch to the tele-election system—one hour before the national voting booths closed."

The other ministers pounded the table jokingly. York's election protest had made the global news networks seconds after it occurred. His profile was laser-beamed around the working and outland world as an "electoral terrorist." The very president whose second term he was opposing had to rescue him from a fanatical flock of E-POLI agents. They had practically besieged Sualouiga City and sought to maul his

Middle Region district in less than an hour, looking to haul the senate hopeful off to their notoriously swift tribunal in Paris.

"Well, today we have TeleVote Nine Hundred," smiled York with a sheepish grin. "Now all people need is the nine hundred number prefix and a retina scan to vote from their home, office, or car, through their computer, vidphone, or television. It is the norm."

"And so, ladies and gentlemen, viral feed is one of our norms," added the president. "It is not on this morning's agenda, nor are the questions of people's access to administration raised by my good Minister Méran.

"What we do have, foremost, are nervous bankers with whom to teleconference by week's end, who will then air-bus from Brasília and Mandela City in less than two hours to seal agreements with us in Sualouiga City.

"I need," emphasized the president by slapping her palm-size vidphone closed, "to finish our position on this port matter today, before I meet with the select committees on finance, trade, and transbloc relations! Need I remind anyone that one of those committees is headed by our able opposition, and that our transbloc relations are coordinated by the chief pest of that consortium of Cole Bay and South Quarter independents?"

Special relations were exactly what Lakshmih knew, in that vid instant, would be her key to further open the explorations for union. Converging were Brazil's weighty NAFTASPHERE presence and South Africa's growing transbloc holdings. The latter country was committed to heading off the West African Federation from opening its second trans-Ethiopian Ocean route between its European Union/Africa portal and NAFTASPHERE by investing in the Trans-hemispheric Port's sub-extension. With the Federal Republic of Benelux in the mix, it was already proving to be another delicate, often ugly, but always obscenely profitable trade tirade played out in the duty-free city-island.

President Lakshmih had by now become obsessed with the dream of union for her land. Her immortality was surely fated by the electoral mandate.

"We have the wealth of post-modern pharaohs," her business backers drove into her, time and time again. "With the national integrity of our now divided land in our hands, we will eclipse all the city-islands." They would ramble on, mixing the long portfolio of her bloodline, the real-earth-politic pragmatism of her government, the populist mandate, and what appeared to be their desperate ambition to be rid of the French's attempt to bar them from integrating total island wealth. Her backers were also better positioned to lead than the North's small pampered native elite and mass of dispossessed.

In all of this, Lakshmih could hear her grandfather's admonitions left on XXX-speed CD-ROM, DVD, and 3-D hologram bytes and taught in high school political science classes: "Our presidents must beware of personal obsessions of aggrandizement in the new age, postmodern democracy. Our business sector, whenever it can remain ours, and ours it must be, is soul bound to be an eternal flame to sponsor national integrity in prosperous harmony with globalization. Neither pylon must ever engage in desperate ambitions that are bound to clash with the powers of the transblocs."

President Akillah Lakshmih envisioned herself the catalyst of a unity articulated by increasing numbers of successive generations spread over a century.

"Dr. Arrindell, welcome. Please sit next to me."

"President Lakshmih, my honor."

"You didn't threaten a viral feed did you?"

"Unthinkable."

"I thought so much of that rumor."

"It is the real terror of our age. The rumor has become a spiteful tool of the earth citizen-consumer in the global marketplace. Our people foresaw this predicament of freedom centuries ago, when they said 'A liar is worse than a thief.'"

"Dr. Arrindell, what is so pressing this time?"

"This, my president," said the scientist in a covert tone. He inserted the two-inch DVD CD in the slot of his upgraded turn-of-the-century IBM ThinkPad. He passed the portable computer with an air of utmost confidentiality to his leader.

President Lakshmih read the abstract. The Egyptian-cut of shoulder-long locks pulled heavily from her skull. "This," she thought stoutly as her eyes scanned the text, "must become the key to special relations." She composed the quickening of her eyes behind the rimless glasses to an interrogator's stare. "I am not a scientist, Dr. Arrindell. What exactly is this?"

"It is what it says it is! To put it in good old Sucker Garden English, we can suck out air from fire. We can put out any fire in a vid instant. By creation, Madame President, we can cool a volcano under the sea with a few more years based on what we know at this moment."

Lakshmih passed the wise-worn laptop to the premier scientist.

"Our families go way back," he said and punched the delete button. The abstract winked off the paper-thin FED screen.

"Our blood knows this island for over three hundred years. It is said that you even know your father's distant ancestress, a little girl who came cramped on the slaveship Snellheid Willem II. Was it in the year seventeen hundred and eleven?"

The president nodded respectfully and headed off the scientist's penchant for historical recollections to get to a current point. "Dr. Arrindell, our families have another history together."

"Yes," he smiled. "Your great-grandfather went against the odds, and took the independent risk of those who become truly great. When my grandfather approached him with the Translinxx idea it was scribbled on crumpled Kwanzaa gift paper. The cost to develop the prototype was nearly the same as the national budget then!"

"I heard about that."

"Yes, my president. It nearly brought the

first national government to an inglorious end."

"Yes, yes," gaveled the president impatiently.

"But our founding father kept the development of the Translinxx chute for St. Martin. People ridiculed him and it. They asked, "why do we need to go from Sualouiga City—it was Philipsburg then—to Marigot in less than three minutes nonstop at moderate speed?"

"Today the old paved route from the capital to the Union Road frontier complex and on to Marigot is used for jogging, national and regional bicycle races, Jouvert, and the Grand Carnival Parade. It is a garden-lined parkway for lovers and spectators. I still think our artists are overdoing it with all those sculptures, eh? The Translinxx shoots overhead in its fiberglass tube. It has made the city virtually auto-free.

"How did it all happen?"

President Lakshmih nodded to the scientist's rhetorical question, anticipating the answer she already knew.

"The president got a consortia of St. Martin, ACS, NAFTASPHERE, and other investors together. Some still question the price he supposedly paid for some of that money."

"Well, rumors persist," egged on Lakshmih.

"Our ancestors were practical men, child."

The president flicked her right eyebrow high. She realized then how long it had been since the eminent scientist and beloved family friend had last called her "child."

"The Translinxx made our country and families stinking rich from the export of the motor module alone. Then we added the power-saving, suprex conductor quad-energy solar chiplex."

"Your contribution, doctor," offered the chief executive with a sort of kindergarten pride.

"Yes, yes. I was at Kyoto University when I led my classmates into that Nobel Prize-winning development. Our suprex conductor solar chiplex is still the best in the world, our greatest export. The very air-buses use it to obtain cruise control in earth and lunar orbit tourism."

"We are a blessed nation."

"This new development will bless us sevenfold. Madame President, I want my country to develop FireVex. The investment will be inordinate. The returns pharaonic. Immeasurable. You can open the powerful investment doors. Rumors or not, you know how to protect the development until we enter the market.

"You know how it is today. A few lead-market months will secure a pylon's edge for a few years."

The sixty-five-year-old scientist got up and took leave of the president. He moved as if his mind had been sentext to his University of St. Martin laboratory and was beholding the prototype.

This invention, President Lakshmih thought, will be the payment for union. But how would she convince the Arrindell family, the nation, to sell out this probable fortune to the French, and to sacrifice the genius of a most lauded son?

How would she . . . could she? Her near orgasmic stream of thoughts was broken by the slight limp of the scientist re-entering her field of vision. He silently leaned over the threshold, leaving the door wide open. Her thoughts returned, sighting the opening to immortality in an age when a lasting national triumph was as hard won as a global one.

SBZT . . .TIQUE, interrupted the fleeting pinioning sound of a micro sub-sentext. She composed herself, stood at attention, confidentially walked to her desk, seated herself as if to give a state of the nation address on E-News/SMCTV.

"Enter," she ordered. The executive communications desk monitor displayed an executive e-mail advisory from the French president: THE FRONTIER WILL BE CLOSED FOR NATIONAL SECU-

RITY REASONS, it read.

Since the hurricane of 1995, the French State had become accustomed to closing and opening the frontier for some national security reason or the other. This was the first such advisory of her term, and President Lakshmih would make formal inquiries through St. Martin's ambassador in Paris. She issued a visual micro subsentext.

"Ambassador Jarvois-Jeffry, I can hear E-POLI and sundry scraping the fibers and Internet already. What is happening over there now?"

"Madame President, the London fires might be spreading," answered the usually curt emissary.

"I know what time it is there, but surf cyberspace and official channels. Come home tonight St. Martin time. Brief me and prepare abstracts for Cabinet." Lakshmih's blood was aboil. Something was abrew and, she sensed, overripe for a feast of fortune at her side of the bargaining table. Had she thought a moment before about selling out her own country's invention to buy back another part of her mothernation? Was she thinking of assaulting the edifying force that the old scientist had become for his country and the Caribbean?

London was the first of two European Union cities scorched by the scourge of nations: narco-terrorists, or "The Terror," as the illusive mercenaries and their drug czar sponsors were called.

It was rumored initially that NAFTA-SPHERE bankers had ignited the infernal sky-red to weaken the 22-member European Union. E-News:/*Time* held sway with its version: London bankers had led an unexpected offensive that was succeeding in routing South American narco-lords from lucrative inter-EU trade trenches. The assault, however, favored tax-free trade escorts by narco-shoguns into far Eastern transblocs and desperately polarized Asian and Pacific outland countries.

The banking barons of the city, whose very financial foundation was steeped in the molten mead of blood and bones from the historic trans-Atlantic European slave trade, set E-POLI with corrosive glee on the tails of unsuspecting and "alleged" Terror chiefs. For this, London was leveled by unquenchable fire. For malicious measure, Madrid too. The latter, after it refused refuge to the running bandits en route—it was rumored—to the Quisqeyan or to the Bahamian Republic.

The president sought her country's region of advisors at home and from around the working and outland world.

Hours later, as Ambassador Jarvois-Jeffry entered the Presidential Suite, the chief executive was ending an audio micro sub-sentext.

"Dr. Arrindell, I believe our ancestors called it 'dancing with the devil.'"

"Uh-huh. Uh-huh. Yes, yes, indeed, and we know full well how often our ancestors had to out-dance the devil," she concluded.

The ambassador's brief confirmed the information that the president had been collecting throughout the afternoon and evening. His detailed report elaborated: Narco-terrorists had informed the French government that Paris would burn in two days if E-POLI, headquartered there, would not release its coven leaders who had been swiftly pressed nine months ago by E-POLI into APIT, the Alpine Prison for International Terrorists. Other landmark EU cities would also be consumed in blazing revenge in what the French secret service code-named: "Firespill."

Ambassador Jarvois-Jeffry was spirited back to Paris that same night with one directive: Begin negotiations for the North.

Events, trends, and conditions, the handmaidens of great opportunity, were gracefully kneeling, heads bowed, hands outstretched, palms upturned, before the luck of Lakshmih, waiting to be sent forth with her bidding.

The president summoned her Cabinet. Following a grueling meeting, the ECM, with the exception of the minister for internal affairs, dispersed swiftly to attend their respective duties. Méran's DVD memoirs, published years later, recorded "ministers dispersing starkly hushed-mouth. So much like the convention of cardinals after the pontiff conceded the Vatican's loss of the Latin American church to the Aristidian monks fortressed in their Machu Picchu citadel of post-liberation theology."

The chief of security services was summoned. The three, attended by a crack side of advisors, conferenced until dawn. Their last decision was coded confidential.

"The ancient Chinese said, 'Preparedness against the unexpected is a way of good government.' Congratulations, my dear and beloved president," confided the security chief with a hand salute over his heart. He took leave to engage his country's duty and destiny. The minister for internal affairs also took leave with the grand sense of purpose.

Sleeping moles were awakened in the North's heartland. French secret agents throughout the island were tagged. Security movements were monitored, allies were alerted, and other portfolios of strategies opened.

It would be rumored not long after that moment that the minions that Lakshmih's great-grandfather supposedly called upon to help secure the first years of independence from a predatory neighbor, were roused again from their laser-fortified golden lairs in Cali. They were to be part of the outer perimeter of protection for Dr. Arrindell's invention and the minds surrounding it—for a considerable cut.

"Now," breathed the sleepless president as she spun alone dreamlike in her throne-comfort seat of power, "from here we will hold the French by their pompous hairy seeds."

"My God, President Lakshmih! You look like a wild something! You'ain gone home since yesterday? Woi ahl yu people treat the human body so? You wahn some Yvette's Bush Tea? That's your favorite, I'll . . ."

"Good morning, Jennifari! Tell me something . . ."

"Oh no! I hear that advise-me-on-this tone.

I do not want to give no more advice on state matters. Last time you didn't take my advice, and the St. Lucians got the lead in that research to blow out gales before they reach hurricane strength."

"Jennifari."

"Then ahl yu laugh when I told you don't leave the West African Federation use the country to smuggle back African art from EU. Everybody knows the 'Star of Africa' diamond passed through here to Abuja before the London fires. Ahl yu' keep playing with E-POLI and we will see poverty when they brand us 'outland'. . ."

"Jennifari," gave out the president with a calming sisterly tone, "what price would you pay for St. Martin, for the North?"

As if not grasping the question's gravity, the receptionist answered without pause. "Madame President, we were friends since high school. My head was too hard to go past two years University.

"Your father gave you his brains and everything else, except his name. Even I only know the rumors about your mother's people rejecting him.

"You come back from the United Caribbean University and that Ivy League place in the

States. Then you set up the School of Caribbean and American Language Studies at USM and you became the darling of intellectuals, artists, and just about everybody else. I wondered, when would you find time for us to be friends again? Then you come to ask me if you should run for president, I really fall out meh skin."

The middle-aged woman approached the pre-sidential desk as one would to a secret to which a life had to be sacrificed for it to be contained. Her voice lowered to a whispering tremble. "We don't lime like school days, but when you ask me to be your receptionist, I felt you wanted to let me know that real friendship is also about trust. For me, working with you has been the happiest time of my life."

The voice trebled to familiarity.

"When you tell me block E-POLI's super secret sentext, especially those subs and micros, it's like I am president of the St. Martin Republic." Both women smiled mischievously.

"When you say, 'Jennifari, I need your advice,' I does really get the shitting. Sometimes I does get real vex."

Both women raised their right eyebrow like an arrow shot skyward. That was proof during school days that they were "sisters."

"One of my great, great-grandmothers was in this union thing. I have one of the first unity flags she had. I doan know why I is the one this flag stay with, just like this union thing stay with the people. We all have something for it in we blood, but t'ain everybody a leader or brave like One-Tété Lohkay and those other heroes we learn about in school.

"Everybody doan care or dance the same time, even when it a family band playing. You ask me what price I would pay? I voted for you! You better ask me, Madame President, what price you should pay, becausin it is you who . . ."

"What price should I pay for One St. Martin, Jennifari?!"

The friend took aim at her leader, raised her eyebrow with piercing defiance. "Dance with the devil, Akillah. Give them fire and brimstone."

With the same defiance, Jennifari spun away from the desk. Walking away, her mango-sweet-shaped behind swaying, she inquired with an old prudish formality, "So, I take it, it shall be a cup of Old Yvette's Classic Bush Tea Mix, Madame President?"

Lakshmih, spinning like a whirlwind of madness, answered starkly, "Ahl yo' full well know, da's all Oi does drink on a good S'maatin morning."

But all things of mice, men, and women were minced before maturation in this age. Just eighty years earlier, most state secrets took months or even years to be leaked, alleged, and unlocked. In this time, they could be accessed, cracked, and revealed by any number of interactive multimedia systems—from vidphones to Earth-Net-linked personal computers—in hours, minutes, and even nanoseconds.

"The vengeance of the masses," is what USA President Nathanial T. Powell called the inability of post-modern governments, corporations, and militaries to hold on to secrets for too long. Hackers and ordinary citizens seemed to take dutiful delight in exposing high level secrets. Hacking had become "the David stone," dealing the most unceremonious blow to the nation state.

The dismantling continued as if vengefully through the reign of assiduous trading transblocs, transnational banking cartels, the sometime, shadowy, but generally restrained, professionalism of E-POLI, and the simple fact that over three and a half billion people—at last count—just relished tattling to each other practically every second. They kept the E-Net, World

Wide Web, and their virulent tributaries a perpetual racing deluge of human issues with translator modems at a steamy full red.

This tattling was cemented by trading of everything from Afghan carpets, Chinese proto-techno secrets, Zimbabwean super-grow vegetables, German short-range hovercrafts, Fijian *haute cuisine* fish, rare red diamonds from abandoned Martian mines, to Rubén Darío's poetry. The latter, with experimental DNA voice cloning of the long-dead Nicaraguan personage, had surfaced as an insatiable fad in Dai Nippon the previous year. It had been spreading like a viral feed ever since.

In this time, small, prosperous city-states and city-islands, able to move everything and everyone faster than transblocs, and more openly safe than the less regulated, but incessantly warring outland countries, became the proverbial sprat. St. Martin was the uncontested *doña* of the sprats, able to lead whales to feed without being consumed in the unrelenting frenzy of the planetary and lunar market.

Not long after the president inhaled the tea's sweet warm aroma in her air-conditioned penthouse office that looked across Great Bay Harbor from the national government complex on the Little Bay Peninsula, E-News Headline @8:15AM stated that The Terror would strike Paris in less than forty-eight hours. Headline @8:30AM had two optional download sidebars. They flashed on the Presidential Suite's wall-flushed FED monitor: CALI GOLDEN MERCENARIES ON THE MOVE! and FRENCH HAVE FORMULA TO FOIL FIRESPILL!

Lakshmih's vid glared for response. She was silent.

"Jennifari, my girl," she audio sentext.

"Yes, my president?"

"Hold everything and everyone. New security codes were issued this foreday for emergency executive contacts. I am going home to freshen up and . . ."

"Sleep?"

". . . rest."

President Akillah Lakshmih rose from her seat like an elegant gale and sent her hands into a clasp behind her back. With her head down, like a pensive ancient, she moved to the stained cedar and polished brass in-laid window. She tipped its fingerprint sensor latch. Before her finger withdrew, the large window parted slightly in half and silently gushed open.

The sea breeze soothed away the tiredness

from her eyes. She surveyed the stirring city. She sensed her people were as calm as the pinkish glow that was buffing the landmark Great Salt Pond this blowing season.

Then she felt the jeweled eyes of the figures peopling the colossal hill-high monument overlooking the hemispheric port and Caribbean Sea from Pointe Blanche. The eyes were intently upon her. The morning sun slowly turned the hillside into a dancing prism of glass, granite and marble, silver and gold. The diamonds donated by South Africa for the ancestral eyes, because of the sun's good morning angle, glittered a subdued angelic brilliance.

The monument was as a *tonnelle* to those consumed by shark jaws in the abyss of the Caribbean Sea and what was called the Atlantic Ocean back then, to those consumed without funerary dignity during the unholy centuries of slavery and indenture, and to those tortured until death by the whip across the salt ponds, on the vast plantations, up in the sumptuous mansions, and down in the mines of the western hemisphere.

When it was unveiled, ten years after independence, DVD and CD-ROM school texts and E-Net tourist brochures state, that the steps were wet with tears for days from the thousands of pilgrims. Throngs stood in processional lines to pay their last respects, to rest the ancestors in peace, and to seek atonement.

Since the ancestral monument was stood on high, descendants of the enslaved, maroons, and indentured, folks from original homelands, and those seeking reconciliation for the souls of their fathers and mothers who had died with the whip in their hands and evil in their hearts, had been making their pilgrimage in the millions.

The president would visit the holy place this morning, offer a prayer, and leave a flamboyant bouquet on the pyramid of steps under the eternal flame. She could, she thought, ask forgiveness too, for claiming so swiftly, so selfishly, the ambition that sought to make the sweet land whole while at the same time souring the very soil worked by ancestors and to be walked on with innocence and pride by the nation's future. Was modesty given due audience? Did strategy give thorough thought to justice for all and duty to nation when opportunity for gain was grasped in the force of momentum and sudden rapidity?

She knew, now, that to claim immortality one engaged an unspeakable inner *boulé-zin*. Yet, she would continue to arch her back under the limbo's ordeal of fire. She felt like the mare on which divine horsemen rode through that night in which one must weep for joy to come in the fine morning. She would be the rainbow over which a pageant of generations would cross to reclaim the whole Sweet Land.

Before Lakshmih reached her bed, E-News//SM had a new headline: BETRAYAL!

"Audio read," said the president firmly. She continued to blow-dry her tongues of hair.

MARIGOT/E-NEWS.METRO.COM: YVES SAINT-ORLEANS, LEADER OF THE GRAN BLANC PARTY (GBP), MOMENTS AGO SENTEXT TO E-NEWS CENTRAL THAT THE STATE IS ABOUT TO SELL OUT THE METROPOLITAN CONDOMINIUM.

"Off audio. Save all news. Sleep: Four Hours."

President Lakshmih mounted her bed in naught but skin, oiled and perfumed to cool softness. The communications, light, and temperature systems of the presidential house were bio-sensitized, softened, silenced, to her desire. Her fiancé stirred. Her perfume sirened him to awaken. He felt her silken skin of wondrous black. His vid alarm chimed "10AM." Voice mail tumbled through. He ordered silence. The holograms saved were suppressed.

A message-minder slipped out: "Noon meeting for wedding arrangement."

Another message-minder: "Organize report abstracts before convening plenary session of Supreme Court on constitutional parameters for Port's sub-extension."

And yet another: "Reconfigure final constitutional draft notes for St. Martin/Anguilla/Nevis/St. Kitts/St. Barths confederacy."

It was his day off. There was time for all the above.

Into his arms and upon his bosom the chief justice drew his wife-to-be. She appealed backward, eyes closed like blind justice, features divine. Her breasts of pomegranates bloomed at his touch, and the nipples rejoiced to a pouting fullness. He called her name, sweetly, once, twice, thrice. The glean of her skin held him hungrily. His hands carved her as if from Nile valley clay. He caressed the pleading arch of her back down and over goddess moons of ebony. The purple velvet of her lotus rose opened with the greeting of dew upon the lips of dawn. He offered her over upon the altar of Erzulie, and she turned with serpentine grace and breathless cries not to be sacrificed without defense. He descended the sable cutlass of orishan pleasure. Her moist ascent blushed around him as they drowned in the mist and must of mutual ecstasy.

Broad as the noon sun was bright that day, Saint-Orleans ordered a cache of weapons on the E-Net. So did Desa Jacques. His Haitian-descent father—in wake of the Marigot Riviera riots that scattered droves of armed EU settlers back home—had been imprisoned in the Alpine gulag five years ago for authoring a viral feed to Mayor Joshois Walker's office with the words: "One St. Martin Now."

Since then Desa headed the St. Martin Now party. His text-tappers piggy-backed SMN's arms shipment on that of GBP's.

Both groups collected their shipment at midnight-covered sea coordinates. Following slingshots of insults shouted from their fibergenic swifts out at sea, it was not long before SMN and GBP activists were shooting their way into port. There they were met by a now super paranoid PAF-MC. The Metropolitan Condominium frontier security literally laser-splintered both swifts and everyone aboard. Yet hours later, other arms orders went out as brazen as before.

By the end of the week, after port negotiations with the investors, Vice President York was chairing a tri-partisan committee on the port's investment and sub-extension portfolio. Elsewhere, at the old Union Road frontier complex, President Lakshmih was lifting guavaberry to champagne crystal glasses to toast the signing of preliminary agreements with the French head of state for the return of the North. The release of Desa Jacques's father was secured in the mix.

By the time the leaders and their academy of political advisors, corporate captains, leading scientists, and military/security heads were drinking, smiling, and shaking hands as they do on such occasions, E-News had circled the globe, monopolizing news bytes for a rare thirty minutes about THE GREAT SCIENTIFIC BREAKTHROUGH AGAINST MAN'S OLD ENEMY—NOT HIMSELF, commented the third editorial in that rare time span, BUT FIRE!

Before the digital ink had dried on the preliminary agreements, the German-French BIONEXUS firm, Brazilian bankers—rumored to have held the narco-terrorists in their dens with some promise or other—the Arrindell family's Translinxx Earthbound, University of St. Martin, and the soon-to-be-federated St. Martin republic, began consortium plans to develop, robotech, and transmarket the century's invention: FireVex. Dr. Arrindell, with Earthbound's Carib-

Stock holdings and NASDAQ stock in laser drive, conceded to the French demand that the joint product be called Fire-Vector.

Less than twenty-four hours after the sprat led the whale to feed, and while most St. Martiners were bursting into the streets in ecstatic spree, GBP militants were setting liquid explosives along the steel pylons of the Translinxx's northern quadrant. Saint-Orleans, himself in twentieth century battle fatigue, was occupying the old Union Road frontier complex under the center of the Translinxx, affectionately called "Welinxxway." Mayor Walker, who had clinched his last dash to the Mairie's after a rumored secret pact with GBP, was busy working out the profitable portions of the deals for federation.

Desa Jacques and his freedom fighters, equally assiduous, were moving through the Simpson Bay Lagoon, now a nursery of marine abundance. Any minute now they would alight on the lush scenic banks of the historic wetland long declared a Protected Earth Monument by the international greenists' Earth-See Society. His plan was to head his troops for a counter-assault on the Gran Blanc hold-outs to union.

President Akillah Lakshmih, who kept the East Indian religion of her mother and bore the kindly stern features of her father's elegant ebony women, was routed from her silk-sheeted bed by a constant battery of micro sub-sentext upgrades from security, then by a courtesy pre-E-News/SM sentext from St. Martin's bureau editors. All concerned the imminent attack by GBP against St. Martin's union and the country's first technological wonder. Though man-made, the Translinxx had even become an Earth-See tourist attraction. Some say it was a trade-off for giving in to the influential eco-tourist group's lobby to empty the lagoon of yachts and other pollutants rather than succumb to the dreaded greenist embargo.

The nation's first received the news seated on her bed, legs crossed in meditative fold. Smoke from incense lighted not six hours before at the feet of Krishna's black marble image, coiled behind her crown twist of dreadlocks. President Lakshmih sub-sentext both men on their vids. The translator modem blinked feverish red for all who might tap and hack and scratch through to witness the communication.

The Madame President pleaded with both rebels to immediately halt "that barbarous kind of twentieth century hostility," until all parties could meet. She promised "most sincerely" an immediate nationwide TeleVote Nine Hundred to accelerate the consensus principles of federation.

Then she raised a spitfire voice to marble coldness, her body levitated, her eyes stared with hawkish vision through the sweet aroma of holy incense: "And, gentlemen, if any destruction comes to our Translynxx, I self will crush you with a thousand hands."

Glossary

ACS - Association of Caribbean States
ah - of
ahl yo', ahl yu - all of you
ain, t'ain - it is not
asanthane (Ashanti) - king, ruler
bandera (Spanish) - flag
becausin, 'causin - because
Benelux - Belgium, Netherlands, Luxembourg
bienvenue (French), *bienvenido* (Spanish) - welcome
boi - buy
bon nuit (French) - good night
boulé-zin (Haitian) - trial by fire; sacred ceremony to achieve second level of Voodoo initiation
brer rabbit, compa nansi - popular trickster persona of African, Caribbean, African-American folklore, hustler; antecedent of bugs bunny
buh - but
'buse - abuse, verbal abuse, to curse
cahn - can't, cannot
callaloo - green leafy vegetable, used in rice dishes and soups
CaribStock - Caribbean stock exchange
champene - champion
chil'ren - children
chiplex - smaller than 20th century computer microchip, quadruppled capacity
choil - child
chups - sound of sucking one's teeth, in disgust, disagreement
comess - confusion

compadre (Spanish) - godfather; crony

coonoomoonoo - cuckold; a fool

crapo la - frog; awkward, bungling person

Cubaïti - suggesting association of Cuban and Haitian engineers

Dai Nippon - Japan

dem - them

Derio - Thomas E. Duruo (1863-1949), St. Martin orator, Black nationalist, pan-Africanist; a premier Garveyite leader in Dominican Republic, Aruba, St. Martin

dey - they

djab (Kwéyòl) - devil

doan - don't, do not

dushi (Papiamentu) - sweetheart; term of endearment

épée à épée (French) - sword-to-sword, point-to-point; an épée is a sharp-pointed duelling-sword

Erzulie (Haitian) - goddess; orisha or spiritual force associated with the power of love

espérate (Spanish) - wait

EU - European Union

faader - father

faah - far

FED - field-emission display, thinner and with resolution superior to LCD monitors now used in laptop, an advanced computer monitor/screen technology

fo' - for

foind - find

gallo hiero (Spanish) - iron cock (rooster); connotes virility, potency, courage

gigabyte - a computer science term, referring to a unit of information

giol - girl

griot (West African language? French?) - storyteller

guavaberry - national drink of St. Martin
heem - him
hoide - hide
impis (Zulu) - warriors, soldiers
jokey - comic, jester like; comical
jumbies - spirits, ghosts
Krishna (Sanskrit, meaning "black") - popular Hindu deity, sometimes manifest with four arms; eight avatar, or incarnation, of Vishnu
Kurosolenean - Curacaolenean, a person from the Caribbean island of Curaçao
Kwanzaa (Swahili) - feast of the first harvest, a seven-day end of the year celebration in USA and parts of the Caribbean
Kwéyòl (Creole, Patois) - An African as well as European-based "New World" language. Spoken in Haiti, St. Lucia, Dominica, Guadeloupe, Martinique, creoles vary in form, spellings and pronunciation
La Barrière - the gate. In former times, a gate guarded the entrance to the Northern village of Cul-de-sac; visitors, suitors to village girls, had to get permission to enter
la-lwa-di (Haitian) - dance groups' Lenten activity, half profane, half ritual
last lick - a children's game, tag
l'éperon (French) - the man-made spur of gamecocks
leggo - to let go, joyful, carnival-like abandon
leh - let
lewoz - a still-popular Guadeloupean traditional drum dance
lokrio - a popular rice, chicken, and vegetable dish of St. Martin
lowe - love
Machu Picchu - a fortress city of ancient Incas, saddled

between two towering peaks, 80 km NW of Cuzco, Peru
mahga - meager
Mairie - mayor's office and municipal administration building in Marigot, St. Martin
makamba, bakra (bukra) (African language?) - white person, European
maroon - Black man or woman who escaped from slavery and lived free in the forests, mountains, swamps, etc. of the Caribbean and Americas; a traditional reference to picnics and cockfights in St. Martin; also refers to traditional collective building projects in Grenada
Matamba - a West African people from area of present-day Angola; story's reference is to Queen Nzinga (1582-1663)
meh - me, my
mek - make
moine - mine
mudder - mother
NAFTASPHERE - in story, reference is to New American Free Trade Agreement, the transbloc or trade bloc power encompassing countries from Argentina to Canada
nanoseconds - denoting factor of 10^9
NASDAQ - New York-based stock exchange company
ni - nor, neither
oan - own
odah - other
Oi - I
oilans - islands
oize - eyes
oom (Dutch) - uncle
opstandig (Dutch) - rebellious, in an annoying kind of way
orishan (orisha) (West African language/Yoruba?) - literally

"Select Head"; according to A. Fatunmbi's study, various forces in nature that guide consciousness in African-based New World mysticism and religions; an orisha is also called a loa

PAF - French immigration/frontier police

Pasha (Turkish) - chief; military commander; governor of province

PMLA - Philipsburg Mutual Improvement Association, a benevolent association, social club, offshoot of Marcus Garvey's UNIA

Ponum - national dance of St. Martin

primo (Spanish) - cousin; term of camaraderie

pris-des-yeux (Haitian) - clairvoyance; final level of Voodoo initiation

quimbés, quimbé - impromptu, traditional topical St. Martin song, sung in a fast-paced singsong without musical accompaniment

Quisqeya - indigenous name for the Dominican Republic

roight - right

Rosicrucian - a member of 17th-18th century order devoted to occult lore (possibly founded in 1484)

'Rubians - Aruban, person from the Caribbean island of Aruba

Sannemengo, Sannemingo - Santo Domingo, capital of the Dominican Republic, is often used to refer to the entire country

Schoelcher Day - celebrated in Grand Case, St. Martin, to honor French abolitionist Victor Schoelcher

sentext - in story, various forms of official and news communication data; sub and micro sentext are confidential, harder to tap into

Shango - popular orisha of Afro-based New World religions; name of orisha or spiritual force identified with power of lightning, courage, justice; also symbolized by rooster

skiod - scared

S'maatin - St. Martin, Caribbean island

sous-sous (French. Also Yoruba?) - in the Caribbean, money; savings between private group of individuals, also called "partner hand"

souse - pickled pig feet

spaniel - in story, reference to Spaniard

staat - start

Statia - St. Eustatius, Caribbean island

stickfight - an Afro-Caribbean martial arts where each opponent used a long wooden lance/stick (e.g. from the bamboo tree). Probable African origin, with varying European and East Indian influence in some islands. Outlawed by slave and colonial authorities

Styx - a river in Greek mythology, entrance to the underworld

Sualouiga (Island Carib?) - said to be Amerindian name for St. Martin, meaning Land of Salt; in story it is the name of independent St. Martin's capital

suprex - beyond super

tante (Dutch) - aunt

tek - take

televote nine hundred - national elections are conducted by TV/vidphone/multimedia systems after dialing the prefix number 900 followed by the citizen's retina scan

toi - tie

toime - time

tonnelle (Haitian) - reference is to a place or ceremony of atonement; reconciliation between the living and dead

transblocs - powerful trading blocs, dividing/linking world economic markets

ven - when
vidphone - 3in. x 3in., quarter-inch thick telephone that allows you to see who you are talking to; works as multimedia/interactive computer, and can generate holograms
vie - we
wahn - want
welkom (Dutch) - welcome
wha - what
wohl - world
woi - why
woodslave - house lizard with large bulging eyes
wuk - work
wuz - was
Yemoja - orisha or loa of water, sea, rivers
yessah - yes sir
'zépaules (Haitian) - dance of orisha Legba, keeper and opener of gates, trickster, linguist and messenger to other orishas; dance emphasizes rapid shoulder movement

HOUSE OF NEHESI PUBLISHERS ⚜ NEW BOOKS

Amazon.com • spdbooks.org • Ask at your favorite bookstore

37 Poems by Lasana M. Sekou

37 Poems is ... significant, vigorous and radical, ... life-affirming in an age when jaded cynicism often passes for wisdom.
- Dr. Tabish Khair, Aarhus University, Denmark

Sekou's passions do not override his poetry, ... his ability to turn a fine line is seen throughout the book.
- Mel Cooke, *Jamaica Gleaner*

skin by Drisana Deborah Jack

Compelling *(poems)* ... We are all migrants now, children and foundlings of diaspora.
- Darryl Accone, University of Witwatersrand, South Africa

Skin takes us through blanket of night, seaweeds, the embrace of the sea, interrupted sky, and rain storms.
- Jacqueline Goffe-McNish, *State University of New York*

The Angel Horn by Shake Keane

Intimate ... cross-fertilizing characteristics of history. The melodious song of a lifetime.
- Anastacia Larmonie, University of St. Martin

The Angel Horn... is vintage Shake Keane. ... spanning a period of 40 years ... the best of Keane.
- Dr. Adrian Fraser, *University of the West Indies*

Caribbean Studies | Modern Poetry | Comparative Literature

New Books, Nuevos Libros, Bukinan Nobo, Nouveaux Livres

www.houseofnehesipublish.com

Available at Amazon.com. Ask at your favorite bookstore.

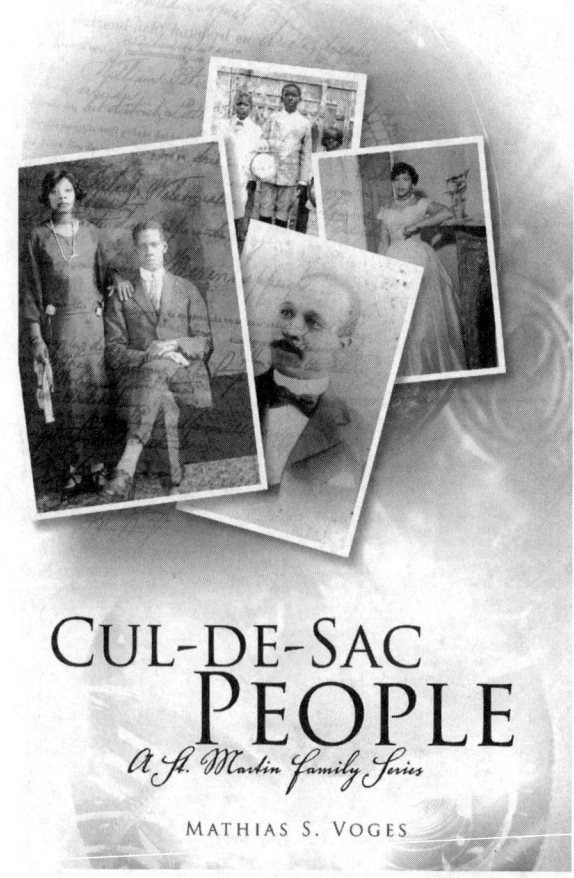

Cul-de-Sac People
A St. Martin Family Series

MATHIAS S. VOGES

Available at Amazon.com. Ask at your favorite bookstore.

In **BROTHERHOOD OF THE SPURS**, a collection of four short stories, Lasana M. Sekou continues his now familiar exploration of the ancestral memory of African Diasporas, which have left their creative imprint on all corners of the Caribbean and the major cities of the American mainland. He can evoke with an astonishing intimacy the pastoral rhythms of an old Ashanti village, or trading city on the eve of European arrival which means rape, pillage, and tragic severances of a people from the veins of an ancient heritage. And all is rendered without any trace of sentimentality or morbid indulgence. It is his skillful interplay of memory and imagination which allows Sekou to take us across oceans and diverse cultures, domestic turbulence and territorial rivalries, without any feeling of rupture or discontinuity in the central theme of the narrative, which is the discovery and collective self-realization of a Caribbean people, whether their acquired identities be with St. Martin, Aruba, Cuba, Puerto Rico, Guadeloupe, Haiti, St. Thomas, Trinidad, Antigua, Saba, Anguilla. There is room for all in this imaginary family, which has made of archipelago probably the first example of a global village. **BROTHERHOOD OF THE SPURS** brings a new dimension to the growing stature of Lasana M. Sekou as a St. Martin and Caribbean writer.

– George Lamming
author of *In the Castle of My Skin* and
Conversations II - Western Education and the Caribbean Intellectual

New Books by Amiri Baraka

the america who dares to challenge the times

Essays • Poems • Available at Amazon.com • spdbooks.org • houseofthenesipublish.com